ROOM 138

JAY WILBURN & ARMAND ROSAMILIA

Madness Heart Press
2006 Idlewilde Run Dr.
Austin, Texas 78744

Copyright © 2021 Jay Wilburn & Armand Rosamilia
Cover by John Baltisberger

First Edition
www.madnessheart.press

Jay Wilburn & Armand Rosamilia

Jay Wilburn dedicates his work in this book to his wife Jenny who is the other half he has always searched for through all of time and space.

Armand Rosamilia dedicates his work to Jay's wife Jenny, the other half he has always searched for through all of time and space. Oh, and his own wife, Shelly, too.

Chapter 1

June 6th, 1987 - Louisville, KY

The woman looked directly at Hank before fleeing room 138.

That was new.

In one hundred and twenty-two ports that he could recall, no one had ever so much as felt him as they brushed against his body, invisible to them and not yet fully there, in the corner.

Invisible to all except this woman.

It took him a moment to compose himself, so shocked at her reaction to seeing him. Surprise, fear, and then panic all hit him.

She'd run from the room, and he had charged after her, catching a glimpse of her flowing red hair as she burst from the side exit into the night.

His satchel slapped against his thigh as he tried to

keep up, but she was fast. Perhaps driven by fear, she was across the parking lot and around the corner of a strip mall before Hank's boots had hit the pavement of the parking lot.

He wondered if going after her or back to the room was more important. He needed to begin his search for the first clue. It was usually in the room.

Another minute passed, but the redhead didn't show herself. She was most likely long gone.

He turned and headed back inside to room 138.

The door was closed and locked. He had no key nor time to finagle one from the front desk clerk. His goal in each instance was simple: find the clues to a room 138 in a certain city. Lie down there, fully clothed, with his satchel and anything else he thought he'd need, and sleep.

He'd wake in another room 138 somewhere else in the world, blended into the curtains or the wall. A few times even as part of the desk.

Always just as the occupants were leaving, the door slamming a few seconds after Hank got his bearings. They weren't checking out. Simply going out for lunch or dinner or maybe sightseeing. Then he'd search for the first clue to the next room 138 he was expected to find. He'd also help himself to any cash or jewelry or anything of value the occupant had left behind.

That would keep him going. The money would be enough to allow him to keep traveling and find the next clue and the next.

It usually took three to five clues that would tell him exactly where he needed to be and how long he had to get there.

Failure to figure out the clues and get to the next room 138 meant something awful. What exactly? Hank didn't know. He just *knew* to miss his next check-in meant he was done.

He also knew no one was able to see him when he first arrived in the room.

No one. Not before now.

The woman hadn't been startled by her shadow or a bug on the wall. In fact, she shouldn't have been in bed at the moment he appeared. She should've been headed out the door. Hank had never caught more than a glimpse of anyone in room 138 unless he'd gone to the door and opened it or saw them from the window.

A greasy plate with bits of onion stuck to it sat in the hallway outside room 140, silverware clustered on one side, and the saltshaker sat on the other with a wadded cloth napkin. No pepper shaker. Either the guy had kept it or the hotel had failed to send it. Either way was weird.

Other than that, no signs of life.

Sure no one was in the hallway this late at night, Hank kicked in the door on the second try. He had little time as nosy neighbors would call the front desk to complain about the noise.

He'd kicked it hard. The lock plate bent away from the door. It pulled nails up from the surface enough to show the rust. Nails and not screws? What kind of sideways establishment was this?

Inside the room he found his clue and something else.

The clue was a simple one: June 15th circled on a small desk calendar. He recognized it easily. More importantly, though, was the satchel at the foot of the bed.

Identical to the one he carried.

Down to the red pin fastened to the strap with a small horizontal blue line with the white numbers 138 on top of the blue.

Hank opened the flap, expecting to maybe see an identical set of items like he carried. There was no real reason to expect that, but he had never seen another bag like his.

Instead, he found a matching set of bra and underwear, a .22 pistol, and two Bowie knives. Sixteen dollars in cash, all singles and from various years: the earliest was 1957 and the latest was 2034.

Nothing else.

He took the second satchel too and rushed out of the room.

"Excuse me, sir," said a small man with thick glasses coming down the hallway wearing a hotel uniform. He wore a big button that was in bright clashing colors from the uniform, on the opposite side from his nametag. The nametag read: Randy. The gaudy button read: Ask me about the Big Horn Lake Eat Local -- Grow Local

Festival.

It took everything in Hank not to ask.

"I'm in a hurry. My wife will pay for the damages," Hank said over his shoulder. "Good day."

Whatever else the man said was lost to Hank as he left the hotel carrying two satchels and ran across the parking lot, hoping to see the redhead but knowing she was long gone.

Maybe she had some answers for Hank.

Like… what was his real name? During a very early port, he remembered one of the clues had been about a recently deceased man named Hank Smith, who'd purchased a lot in the Bowery section of New York City. The year was 1899.

On the next jump, he found out the property still existed. It had been a small storage space, one level, with only a front door and no windows.

He'd assumed Hank Smith's identity and, with forged documents and a lot of money exchanging hands, the storage unit was now his go-to place when he needed to keep something important or bigger than he could carry.

But he didn't know who he really was. He didn't know if the first port he'd remembered was truly the first. He'd learned what little he knew on the fly. Sometimes he suspected he had missing time between clearer memories.

Instinctively, he always knew what year he was in, what city, and the day and time.

He knew everything but who he really was, and why he kept porting from place to place, year to year, seemingly random and without purpose other than to find the next clues to port again.

He needed to find the redhead, knowing "a needle in a haystack" didn't begin to capture the story of how hard that was going to be.

Searching a haystack in every year, Hank thought.

With renewed purpose, he went in search of the second clue.

Chapter 2

June 15th, 2003 - Baltimore, MD

Hank had roughly two months to stay in town, if he had the clues right this time, with no idea how he'd be able to afford it. Getting a job on the docks was one option. He had a faint notion he'd done it before either in Baltimore or the surrounding area. After 2001, he had to have better papers for getting jobs or traveling in some cases. Not sure why, but that's how it worked. The same was true about licences and identification starting about the mid eighties forward. From the 1960's back, it was easier to assume any identity he wanted.

He'd need to be careful and take better notes. Unfortunately, after so many ports, his writing, even though brief, took up three notebooks. Soon he'd need to head to the Bowery and store them.

Unless his next destination was across the country, Hank would need to keep his eyes open for the remaining clues and hope he had enough time.

There had never been a clue that showed up days or weeks ahead of schedule, allowing him some breathing room. Not one he recalled picking up on anyway. It was always last minute and forced him to hustle in his travels, dropping everything at a moment's notice.

He'd been drinking since noon, and that always set his mind to morose thoughts. Sitting at the end of the bar, watching smiling couples come in and out had gotten him down.

One lone man sat in a far booth reading a library book version of Brian C. Redd's 2002 release *The Train to the Salt Lake Wastelands*. He could tell it was the library bound version because it had that weird cellophane wrap over the regular dust jacket that bent up inconveniently when the book was open.

Did people still go to the library in 2003? When did anyone read library books in bars?

Hank couldn't remember if he had read that one or not. It was hard to remember. Reading passed a lot of time for him. Redd was an author he liked. The guy started writing in the early sixties and kept putting out books as late into the future as Hank ever traveled. He kind of suspected the Brian C. Redd name had become a pseudonym for some publisher using lots of different ghostwriters, at some point.

Redd started out with pulp crime and mystery stories. Then, he touched on some sci fi and horror in the 70's and 80's. The work was all over the place after the 90's.

Hank's favorite was a straight up spy thriller that went back to Redd's roots, *The Couple from Nowhere,* that Redd put out in late 2005 or early 2006, if Hank remembered right.

It had a great first line. That book started out simply with "that was new." After that, he had to keep reading to see what happened.

"So, what happens next?" he muttered to himself.

Now that he was thinking about it, he couldn't recall if that was actually the first line of a different book.

Hank never, never trusted his memory.

His last twenty dollar bill on the bar, he knew he'd need something to eat soon. He'd wisely paid the hotel tab for the next week, but that and the afternoon drinking left him with only a few singles.

Ironically, his satchel was stuffed with over two thousand dollars, but the cash wouldn't be printed and in circulation for years.

He spied a saltshaker next to the margarita machine.

"But no pepper," he whispered and smiled.

Someone walked up to the bar, ordered a Rusty Nail, and left with it, ice clinking in the glass as an old familiar tune. The guy paid and tipped with all two dollar bills.

What year had those come out?

Hank stared at the bartender as the man studied the money. The guy smirked and put them away. Maybe a curiosity, but perfectly fine for 2003.

Hank had to make sure he never slipped up and

entered something into a time period that didn't yet exist. He didn't know the repercussions, but it wouldn't be good. He'd seen enough time travel movies to know a 2020 penny given to a street urchin in 1887 would somehow unleash dinosaurs or zombies on the world. Watching TV or going to movies helped pass the time when he had it. Live sporting events were interesting, too.

Maybe he'd go to the baseball game tonight, kill a couple of hours, wander the stadium, and see if a clue appeared.

The TV over the bar showed highlights of a game: Orioles versus Brewers. It had been a day game, and the Orioles had won.

Hank shook his head.

"Not a hometown fan?" said an older woman sitting next to him at the bar. She'd been there for nearly an hour, head down, and sipping beer.

Hank knew the look and sound of someone who wanted to talk, but he didn't want to engage. He wanted to relax. He needed to clear his head and figure out a few things.

But he also knew a truth about himself.

He was lonely.

"I wanted to go to the game. I had no idea it was an early one."

"Baltimore needs to get on a roll. A couple of series sweeps and they could overtake the Yankees and Red Sox this year." The woman held up her beer mug and smiled. "Don't be surprised if they are in it all this year."

Hank shook his head. "Marlins will win it all over the Yankees. Four game to two. Bet on it."

She shook her head. "You're nuts."

Hank shrugged. He'd been in future years and at one point had tried to get a list of winners he could make sure bets on in the past. It hadn't worked out yet. He'd purchased a thousand dollars worth of bets for the Mets in the 1986 World Series, and he knew they had won for over ten grand.

Except he hadn't been to the right part of 1987 or back to '86 yet to collect. Did the tickets expire in Vegas? He also hadn't been close to Vegas in a few ports, either.

It seemed easier when he was putting it all together, but executing anything meaningful took too long.

Hank kept glancing at the door.

"Waiting for someone?" The woman finished her beer and pushed the glass aside.

"Yes," Hank answered truthfully. He'd been watching for the redhead to make a grand entrance and either shoot or kiss him.

He didn't know his real name or where he'd come from. His parents. His childhood. Any memories before his first port.

Hank did know he liked redheads, though. And this one was really pretty from the glimpse he'd had of her before she ran off.

"I'm waiting for someone, too. My husband." The woman smiled. "He went to the bathroom and hasn't returned."

Hank glanced over his shoulder. "Maybe he has stomach issues."

She shook her head and smiled. "He went to the bathroom three years ago. I come back here every day and just sit. I know the owner. The bartender keeps me company when he's not busy. I hold out hope that someday he'll return with a valid excuse. He always had an answer."

Hank made a mental note to return to this bar at a later date and see if she was still at the bar.

As if it was that easy to do. While the days themselves moved in a strict order, it was the year that changed. Today was June 15, 2003, but if he ported tomorrow it would be June 16th 1945 or 2033. It could be any year, even one he'd previously been to before.

Hank wished he had a dog as a companion. Didn't every hero have a sidekick to travel with? He hated not talking to people for long stretches at a time. Maybe with a dog he could talk to it and the dog would tip his or her head in confusion at his rambling. Even sniff out some clues for him.

A bench with a Las Vegas advert? Good boy! Let's catch a bus.

"You have a nice day," Hank said and finished his drink. The bartender had made change and he left a dollar tip, pocketing the rest. He'd need it. "I'm Hank."

She smiled. "Mary."

A puppy would be nice. Then I could carry him in the

second satchel and sneak him in and out of hotel rooms, Hank thought.

He wasn't sure if he'd ever had a pet before.

Hank wasn't sure of a lot of things. He'd binge-watched time travel Netflix movies one weekend, hoping to find a clue or some ideas.

They never show you the mundane days. The lonely days. The times you wonder whether this is worth it or not, he thought.

There had to be a kennel nearby. There usually was in a big city. A local would know. He'd watch for someone walking a dog or someone nice.

Someone who he could have a conversation with.

Now he wished he'd stayed in the bar and talked to the woman waiting for her husband, even if she seemed a little off. Thinking back, she'd looked familiar. Not stunningly so, but like maybe he might have known her younger. Maybe he had.

Mary? Mary. It was going to stick in his head for days.

He needed someone to talk to. A companion. A confidant. His backup during trouble.

Hank And His Time Traveling Dog.

He walked down the street carrying two satchels with two matching buttons, doing more thinking than paying attention for the clues he needed in order to survive.

Chapter 3

July 4th, 1977 - Myrtle Beach, SC

Oh, for the love of … Hank hoped he was right as he thought, *maybe I'm wrong.*

The hotel room wasn't even finished. There was a bed frame, but no mattress. The walls were unpainted with the white splotches for the drywall studs still showing. The work was shoddy, with nail heads oxidizing where they hadn't been covered properly. There were no mirrors, no shower curtain, and no drapes over the window. Morning sunlight blazed in over the ocean at an angle to this room 138.

The half empty bottle of cleaner and the bucket of plumber's putty were on the floor next to the tiled shower. Hank could still smell the chemicals from whoever had been working in here before he arrived. On the back of the bottle, someone had circled, in thick black marker, the words "Let stand for 3 hours before removing."

That sucked. That sucked bad. If this was the clue, then the next port better be within Myrtle Beach or he might be screwed. He wanted to believe the marked bottle was a coincidence and another clue waited outside, but part of him just knew. It was too inconvenient not to be true.

Still, he rolled the drum of plumber's putty over to look for another time limit. He wasn't sure what he expected to find. *Oh, just kidding, Hank old buddy. Let this putty sit for two weeks and then off to Vegas for the plumbers' convention.*

The address of the company that made the putty was in Toledo, Ohio. The company was Red Savannah Seal. It had a lion on an African grassland under the name. If Toledo or Savannah or Africa were where he needed to go in three hours, it was game over. The cleaner's "flavor" was Ocean Breeze.

He took up both satchels and walked through a plastic sheet into the unfinished hallway of the hotel. He didn't bother to try the elevator as he took the stairs.

It was muggy without air conditioning, and he could smell the salt on the ocean air.

As he went through the dusty lobby, some guy in a suit pointed at him. "Who are you?"

"Sorry. I thought this was my hotel. All these places look the same."

"Hey, get out of here."

"Will do."

The guy started to follow. "Hey, come back here."

Make up your mind, chump. I got less than three hours before I have to remove myself.

Hank hit the sidewalk and kept going under the scaffolding where two workers installed a sign a couple stories up for The Dayton House. He continued along the oceanside sidewalk of the boulevard. His eyes darted back and forth searching for the words "Toledo" or "Ocean Breeze" or "Lion" or "Red" or anything. If his time was really ticking down from three hours this time, he'd have to find the clues quick.

He stopped out in front of a small pancake house: Mama's Old Country Griddle. No help there. The pitched roof and the interior in orange, brown, and cream screamed 70's to him. Each decade was like its own planet sometimes. Other times it was tough to tell the difference between the early nineties, the mid eighties, or the early 2000's. The pancakes were screaming at his empty belly, but he was closing in on two-and-a-half hours before the deadline.

He left the pancake house and left Ocean Front Boulevard. He turned on Ninth and turned again.

A micro amusement park lay quiet to his left in the morning light. A few workers in white suits gathered trash from the night before. A giant clown spread a toothless smile on the Tip-A-Whirl and a cardboard Colonel-Sanders-looking-dude leaned back with his hand out under a speech bubble which read: I Do Declare! Little Rebels Must Be At Least This Tall To Ride Rebel Yell Plantation Splash!

Hank thought he should have stayed on Ocean. He felt sure the next clue was about "Ocean Something." Usually he had days or weeks to sort this stuff out.

A movie theater called the Rivoli rose in front of him. He checked out the movie posters behind glass under the shade of the marquee. There were none – just business notices, the Fulton Ironworks was closing, and fuzzy fliers about the fireworks on the beach that evening.

I'm one year off from the Bicentennial, he thought. He had been in Atlantic City for July 4th in 1926, the Sesquicentennial. That was pretty spectacular. Two buildings had caught on fire. Safety standards not being up to later century levels, he supposed.

He craned his neck and stepped back out into the sun. The movies playing were *Herbie Goes to Monte Carlo* and a sneak preview of *The Spy Who Loved Me*. A third notice read, *The Train To.* The "T" and the "O" in "to" were both tilted in different directions. He looked around on the ground for the missing letters.

The train to where? Am I supposed to take a train? Is there a Monte Carlo Motel in Myrtle Beach?

A yellow checkered taxi sat outside the theater a few feet down with the engine running. He could hop in and go anywhere within two-hours-and-twenty-ish minutes' drive, but he didn't know where to go.

His eyes lighted on an old community meeting notice for 1:30 PM on the 8th. One of the topics was "How the Ocean Forest Hotel Debacle Still Haunts the

Beach."

"Ocean Forest Hotel," he whispered. "One-thirty … eighth."

This had to be the clue. He hustled to the cab and opened the back passenger's side door. "Hey, are you waiting for a fare?"

"Always." The man folded his paper and took another sip of a McDonald's coffee. "Just didn't think I'd get one before the first picture let out."

"Great. Can you take me to the Ocean Forest Hotel?"

The guy cut his eyes at Hank and smiled. "Really?"

Hank felt sweaty and itchy under his shirt. He hadn't even checked his clothes for time period appropriateness. They looked pretty plain. That was the safe way to go in most eras. Now he worried the Ocean Forest was hours away based on the cabbie's reaction. "Yeah, can you?"

"Sure … It's not far."

Hank took the satchels off his shoulders and then saw her. She was wearing bell-bottom jeans and a flowered print off-the-shoulder blouse. She looked dressed for the era. Her red hair was twisted up on top of her head, and she had raised her sunglasses up to her hairline. She was staring at him.

He stepped away from the cab to about the back bumper before she backed up two steps and turned her body a quarter of the way toward the amusement park. He stopped short. He opened his mouth to call to her, but then didn't know what to say.

The cabbie called through the open back door. "Hey, buddy, are we going or not? I'm not waiting for you."

Hank said, "Hold your ... Just wait a second. No one else is here right now."

She took another step away even though he hadn't moved. He didn't have time to chase. Maybe she had longer for cat and mouse, but he sure didn't.

He held up both hands like he was calming some rare animal he had spotted in the wild. As far as he knew for sure, they were a rare subspecies of human experiencing time in fits and pieces. They were the only two of their "kind" he knew of for certain.

The satchels swung from his shoulder and bounced against his hip. He had thought about the extra bag a lot over the last few ports. After he ported away from their first encounter, it occurred to him that she might have come back for the bag and found he had taken it. If he left it, he thought she might never find him or talk to him again. Then, he worried that he had left her adrift. There wasn't much to hold onto in their situation.

He'd never been able to port back to a time and place, and wondered if she knew more about this than he did, and if she could teach him a few things. In the least, maybe she could give him some clues about the "clues."

He chewed at his lip as he took hold of the less heavy of the two otherwise identical satchels with their strange matching pins. He hadn't changed anything out including the few dollars she had in there. He held the bag up and set it down on the sidewalk at his feet. She watched him from a distance with wary eyes.

"Movies are about to let out. Am I taking you or someone else?"

Nothing left to hold us together. Good travels, Red.

He thought about the plumber's putty.

He actually waved at her and backed into the cab with her satchel abandoned on the sidewalk.

"You sure about the old Ocean Forest?"

"I don't have a lot of time. Let's go, please."

The cab pulled away from the curb. Hank watched through the back window until they turned. People were coming out of the theater by the satchel, mostly women with kids, but Red hadn't moved from her spot.

They left the beach and cut through neighborhoods until they followed a highway with trees on both sides. They turned up a drive through a break in the woods past a neglected sign for the Ocean Forest.

Hank gathered his satchel, but then the wind went out of him. They made the curve of the roundabout for check-in, but weeds grew up between what rubble remained. A squirrel hopped up onto a jagged chunk of concrete to see who had come to visit.

He opened his door and stood. "It's gone?"

The clue? What had he missed?

The driver said, "I thought you knew. You seemed to know what you were doing. The place never opened. They built it in the thirties, I think, and the guy went bankrupt. It was imploded in '74."

Hank turned in a circle. There were no other signs or scraps of paper lying around. Whatever he had been supposed to see, he had blundered past it. Everything along the beach was probably named "Ocean Something." He had picked up the first random word he found and ran. The fact that she was there in the same city again probably meant the port was close, and he had run away from it.

What now?

He looked at his watch and realized he hadn't reset it for local time. He couldn't have had but maybe an hour-and-a-half left tops.

He drummed his fingers on the trunk.

"I still need my fare, Buddy. I can take you somewhere else, but the meter is running."

Hank lifted his hand to rifle through the bills he had in his bag for everything circa '77 and earlier. He stopped short and stared down at the decal on the quarter panel of the taxi right under him. He had looked at it getting in, but didn't bother to read it the first time. The advertisement was a pastel plantation with rows of oaks draped with Spanish moss. A young couple in Antebellum garb strolled along the path. She had long red hair.

"Where is the … the Fulton Plantation Inn?"

"Um, Georgetown."

"How far? I mean, how quick can you get me there?"

"Forty-five minutes to an hour depending on how

we catch the lights."

Hank hopped back in. "Let's go."

"I need the first fare before we start the second."

Hank dug through his bag. "I'll tip double, if you make it in forty-five instead of the hour."

***

It was closer to fifty-five minutes, but Hank already had the money wadded in his fist. He passed it over and said, "Wait for me as long as this will buy me."

He scrambled out without waiting for a reply and charged toward the converted plantation house. It did not look large enough to have a room 138. If he was wrong again, there wasn't going to be much time for a third try. Missing this time might mean taking the cab to a permanent home somewhere in coastal 1977.

Hank ran into the foyer and turned in a full circle. Two hallways and a set of wide stairs. *So, where to?*

He approached the desk and tried not to give off a serial killer level of desperation. He might be down to minutes at this point. The fellow looked up and painted on the fakest of smiles. "How can I help you, sir?"

"I'm not sure if my party already checked in. I'm booked for room 138, I believe?"

The kid didn't blink as he laid a real key on the counter. "Of course, Mr. Jumper, your lovely wife with red hair for miles said you'd be coming. She left you this spare. She just checked in maybe a half hour ago.

First hallway. Third on the left."

Hank stared for a moment with the key in his grasp. He managed, "Thank you?" And then he ran.

He fumbled the key, and it nearly slid underneath the door. He had to use his thumbnail to pull it back out. He got it unlocked and slammed it closed behind him.

Hank saw her sneakers on the end of the bed from around the corner of the bathroom. He walked up far enough to see her shins, the faded knees of her bellbottoms, and the button on the strap of her returned satchel.

And then she faded. By the time he rounded the corner, her imprint in the mattress was all that was left.

Did I miss the port? Were we supposed to go side by side? It couldn't have been three hours, but it's close. She's gone, and I'm stranded.

Hank saw the folded note written in black ink on both sides of Fulton Plantation Inn stationery.

He snatched it up.

Whoever You Are, I'm taking a big risk leaving this behind, the first line read. *You better be worth it, Stranger. Returning my pack counts for this much, I suppose. If you read this, then we are jumping from the same jump point this time. Maybe we'll cross paths again. I call myself Savannah because it was the first city I woke up in that I remember maybe three, four, five years ago "jumper time?" I pick a different last name every time. I jumped into a Wake Forest male dorm room 138 maybe three weeks ago (that was a trip) (first not real hotel I landed in. Now I wonder if I can show up in an office building conference room 138. Maybe you already know. Maybe I should have trusted you and compared notes before now. Maybe we will someday. I've been hurt by nonjumpers I trusted a couple times in the past. And in the future too now that I think about it.) and got the clue to come to Myrtle Beach just last night. Hopped off the bus to see you standing there with my bag.*

Well, here's what I know, which isn't much. Consider this my thank you for the returned pack, Stranger …

There was more front and back, but there wasn't time. He stuffed it in his satchel and rolled unto the bed right into the impression she left.

Already too late, you idiot. You followed the wrong clue and now you're …

"Just shut up." His voice echoed back at him off the low ceiling.

It usually took him a few minutes to fall asleep. Minutes he might not have if his port time was actually still in the future. He'd cut it close before, but never quite this close. He'd snooze away and then come back around invisible and standing, sitting, or laying in a corner of another room. Incorporeal, really. Then, it was time to steal from the … *Non-jumpers, she had called them.*

He wondered if she had met any others like them. He needed to read the rest of the note, but he needed to go to sleep first. His nerves were wound tight, though.

He guessed she hadn't met any others by the way

she reacted to seeing him the first time. Or maybe she had, and that was why she ran.

"Focus," he demanded of himself.

The exhaustion came over him quickly, like a physical thing, as if he had been injected with something. The room was spinning in his vision and he was going under. Flashes of light exploded from every surface, but he couldn't tell if it was just inside his head.

She had simply faded away when he walked in on her porting. *Savannah. Savannah Jumper, she had called herself this time. She left me a key, just in case this was my port, too. Red Savannah Seal? She ported up in Wake Forest? Maybe I'm getting clues about her now, too?*

The lights smashed through his vision like he was being punched. The rest of the port occurred while he was unconscious, as usual.

Then, he was standing in Room 138 of a hotel in Boston for the Semiquincentennial. A blue foil top hat on the table next to him declared: HAPPY QUARTER MILLENNIUM, AMERICA!

He was focused on other things though.

Chapter 4

July 4th, 2026 - Boston, Mass.

There was a line from a cheesy song about the future being so bright he needed to wear shades. Today it was overcast, and he knew the threat of rain would be met before the fireworks began.

Hank was alone in Boston, but Savannah could be near. She knew a lot more than he did and the rest of the note might shed light on even more, but first he needed to figure out a few things, like food and something to drink.

The year 2026 wasn't filled with cloud cities and AI robots doing the laundry. The furthest he'd gone into the future, or the farthest date he'd ported to, was New Years Eve 2034.

He'd jumped to that date and heard the rumblings of a war coming but he'd never figured the sides and how imminent it was. It could be the United States versus North Korea. Aliens landing in Russia. Canada versus Portugal. Hank had no idea how the planet aligned in that time period.

He was never there more than half a day tops, as far as he remembered. Usually less. Not enough time to figure out the history of the world.

There weren't any hover cars or cyborgs in 2034, either.

Hank wandered Boston's serpentine streets, marveling at some of the same buildings he'd seen in previous ports. Everything he'd ever done was fuzzy around the edges, but he knew he'd walked these avenues before. Whether before he'd been sucked into the vortex of porting or because he'd been here more than he could remember, he didn't really know.

A small park had a free moving train for kids, riding along the sidewalks. The young kids looked excited. Parents varied between amusement at their children's joy or exhaustion. The "conductor" wore a floppy, oversized engineer's cap on his sweaty head. The old man looked dead inside from blowing the whistle from time to time and circling in endless loops.

Hank muttered mostly to himself. "I know the feeling, Buddy."

Tie together children and have faith in God …

Hank couldn't place where the thought came from, what triggered it, or why it mattered. He felt sure he had read it somewhere. Without context, he decided to dismiss it. He'd probably accidentally read it again some day.

Fenway Park was up ahead and when he saw the sign for the Red Sox and their many recent World Series wins, he sighed.

Was it a clue? The color red again. Maybe it was his own wishful thinking because he wanted to find Savannah and pick her brain.

There wasn't a game today and the streets around the ballpark were empty except for normal traffic and workers. He went inside a bar owned by a former Red Sox player and ordered a pitcher of beer and a seafood platter, knowing he had the cash to pay for it in his satchel.

He hoped. It was all a confusing blur sometimes what year he was in and if he had enough, although he'd managed to find three hundred in cash in the room 138 he'd appeared in today.

Sure that no one in the sparse crowd was paying him attention, he pulled out the note and flattened it on the table. He had to move a saltshaker and a napkin holder. Someone had stolen the pepper from the table.

Hank took a sip of beer and read the rest of the note.

Well, here's what I know, which isn't much. Consider this my thank you for the returned pack, Stranger. I've met one or possibly two other jumpers besides you. The one I know for sure, she was anything but friendly. In fact, I believe she tried to kill me. Time travel psychosis? It could be a thing. I feel crazy half the time on a good day. There was one other who I don't think was a jumper, but was involved somehow. I've seen him in more than one time period.

Sometimes I just start to remember something. The pieces are almost together in a way that makes me feel like I should have known it all along. I start to think I'm a bigger part of all of this and in more control than I thought. Then, it slips away.

Someone is after me. Probably after us. Trying to hurt us. If you don't know that yet, you're lucky, but may not be for long. I'm not sure if it is the people behind all this or someone against the people behind all this. Now that I know there were at least three of us, I'm inclined to believe there are more. If there are more, then this is a bigger thing. There might be a reason to have people out there planting guideposts and markers for us. My "friend" (who tried to kill me) used to call them clues. The other guy, the dwarf, did too.

It could just be paranoia though. That would probably be the first symptom of time travel psychosis, if that is really a thing. You should probably disregard everything I said.

Maybe if we meet again, I can explain it better. Suffice it to say, if you've met her (or him) already, you know what I mean. If you haven't, beware the dwarf. Yes, I know that sounds like the start to a bad joke but it's anything but.

Do you have any recollection of when it started for you? I don't. It feels like I was born during a jump. Created? I know that's not correct. I sincerely believe we were "normal" before this happened to us.

We must've been nonjumpers who were thrust into this role. If you think I have the answer to that million dollar question, you're wrong.

I do know about your secret cache in the Bowery because I own a similar property on the same block. I don't think that's a coincidence, either. I think we were destined to meet, but after the dwarf came after me and my friend, I don't know.

We cannot control where we end up, which is going to make this hard for us to meet again. I wish I'd just talked to you on that street, but I didn't know if you were friend or foe.

I really still don't know. You could be working with the dwarf. Or the others.

There has to be even more of us out there. But why?

I guess I don't have the answers you're looking for. I suspect by the look on your face, when we met, you had no idea you weren't alone.

Until we meet again… we'll need to figure out a way to leave messages. I don't suppose getting cell phones and being on a family plan with them would make sense, since we'd be calling from the same day but maybe in different years. I don't know if your jumps line up with mine. That might lead to a lot of missed calls and outdated messages.

I really want to trust you, Stranger. It would make this easier on both of us.

Beware the dwarf… as funny as that sounds.

Savannah

The words squeezed into every line of the paper front and back.

Hank put the note in his satchel, making sure to slide it into a safe spot. It was literally the only thing he owned that had any value to him, despite the money he hoarded.

The restaurant had begun to fill in anticipation of the festivities coming tonight. He supposed many families were having picnics and barbeques at home today. Backyards filled with friends and family, all having a few laughs and good food.

He didn't know if he had any actual family in this world. What if the older couple who'd just sat down a few seats away from him were his actual mother and father? Or his children?! What if the bartender was his sister?

Hank wondered if Savannah was his sister. They looked nothing alike. Yet… there was a familiarity to her. Perhaps he'd seen her before his mind had become a blank slate. What if they had been together for many years before whatever change had happened?

Instead of answering a question, her note had given him more to be confused about. It might've been simpler to think this was all just happening to him. Hank had also seen enough movies to know adding a bad guy to the mix wasn't going to have a happy ending, especially a mysterious dwarf. Or the hallucinations of a woman going mad.

Was he supposed to call them little people? Porting around time didn't help with staying politically correct and "current."

As much as Savannah had warned him about the dwarf, he wanted to see them all. She was another piece to this puzzle. The three of them, the four of them maybe, at least, shared this secret. The ports and jumps and whatever else you wanted to call this. Did the dwarf understand more than Hank or Savannah?

And who was her friend who'd died? Who might have tried to kill her?

He had too many questions and not enough answers. That much was not new.

His head hurt, and he knew it wasn't because of the beer or the growing crowd. He needed to find a quiet spot and think. Tonight would be a challenge to find that spot with all the partying about to blow up.

Hank finished and left, as the line formed on the sidewalk to get inside and spend money and celebrate.

A small boy walked by holding his father's hand. In his free hand, the boy flew a toy train engine over his head like it was a rocket. He pursed out his lips and made a sound like TV static for his train engine rocket.

Hank wasn't in the mood today.

Even before the sun dropped below the horizon, trying to fight through the clouds and incoming rain, Hank heard fireworks in the distance.

He stopped on the street, putting a hand on the wall of Fenway Park and sighed, remembering something from his past. Maybe something from before he began porting. He'd had dreams and short visions in the past, but this one felt well-formed and meant something.

But what?

The sound of fireworks reminded him of gunshots on a battlefield.

I'm about to ask you something very important …

Was that his voice in the memory or someone else?

Rapid fire shooting in the distance, Hank being aware it was getting closer, and there was nothing he could do to escape it. Had there been people with him? Maybe.

We are the same and in a way we were born for this … this choice changes everything …

It was gone in a flash, but so sharp and real he knew it had happened.

When, though? His past, present, and future were all intertwined.

He had no idea what year he was born. Could all the ports be after he was born? Maybe before and he wasn't even technically alive yet.

Hank had spent many sleepless nights wondering who he was. He'd even bought a laptop at one point and searched using facial recognition software, but came up empty.

He didn't exist, but it might've been because of the year he'd done the search. Now he couldn't remember which year it was. The more he thought about the ports he'd done, the more he knew he'd forgotten so many of them. He had visions of certain events he didn't remember, but knew they weren't dreams or nightmares.

Things had happened he'd either forgotten, his mind had wiped them from memory, or something more insidious was going on.

Someone working against us, she'd said.

Hank feared it was the insidious answer.

His journals were incomplete. He knew it now. He'd thought he'd immediately written down every port and every clue.

Something was wiping his memories. Selective memory.

Maybe someone.

Who was Savannah? Really?

It could just as easily be her doing this. Manipulating Hank to do her bidding, whatever it was. Pulling the strings and acting as if she was as in the dark as he was.

Acting like she was also the victim, searching for clues and trying not to get stuck in the same place for all eternity.

He'd never seen her before, and now he'd seen her twice. Both times she'd run away, but conveniently left a note for him to find.

A note which explained nothing.

Savannah might be the reason for his damn life, as mysterious as it was.

Beware the dwarf?

Hank wanted to meet the dwarf more than anything now.

The dwarf might have the real answers.

Now he needed to buy a bottle of something to forget and find a hotel room to get drunk and sleep off this night. He believed it would be a few days until he needed to jump again. Yet, he never knew how he knew.

Hank didn't know a lot of things and had no control over any of it, anyway.

A bottle of Pappy Van Winkle bourbon would hit the spot.

Chapter 5

August 8th, 1993 - Seattle, Washington

Even for Seattle, he was dressed a little warm for August. He always told himself it was easier to remove layers than to steal more to put on later. It had finished raining some time just before he arrived to see a businessman vacating the room, for the morning, ahead of him. He hoped the guy was gone for the morning, and not just grabbing a quick breakfast before returning.

The room was ground floor and slim pickings. The business guy was apparently paranoid about leaving anything of value in the room. Hank stole the guy's toothpaste out of spite. It was some off-brand named Signal.

Hank paused next to the concierge's desk of the Silver Cloud Hotel. Through the water-spotted windows and thin sunshine, it looked about like any other street in any other city.

He adjusted the satchel on his shoulder and whispered to himself, "Beware the dwarf."

"Can I help you with something, sir?"

Hank swallowed and took a step away. The desk sat out in the middle of the floor of the lobby. The fellow had a thick mustache which looked like it belonged a couple decades earlier than 1993. Hank smiled, and the man smiled back. Maybe he was a "jumper," too.

Hank shrugged and said, "Maybe you can. I'm not sure how much longer I'll be in town. Any shows I can catch?"

"As in plays or concerts?"

"Music, I think, this time."

"Forgive me for presuming, sir, but you look a little older than the grunge rock fans who come to town for shows."

Hank had to think. He had checked out music mostly in places where the Internet was available and up to speed. He wasn't sure when the music of his youth would have been from. Some things sounded familiar. Others didn't. He always thought music would be primal, and he'd recognize songs from his own time by feeling. He liked rock, but wasn't sure when "his era" would be, based on what he had listened to. He had caught an Elvis concert in the 50's and a few weeks later a "Fat Elvis" show in Vegas in the 70's.

"I'm open to grunge."

The man shuffled pages on his desk. His golden name tag read Jerry Pine. "Well, let's see who's in town tonight, shall we?"

The guy didn't wear an extra button asking Hank to ask him about local growing festivals. He tried to remember which port that memory had been from.

Hank took a step closer.

"Well, not grunge, but you just missed the Jerry Garcia Band at Memorial Stadium last night. He's gone on to Portland now. What else?"

After a pause, Hank said, "Anyone will be fine, The Doors, Nirvana, Soundgarden, Pearl Jam, Foo Fighters, KISS, Ghost. Anyone really."

"I don't know the Foo Fighters or Ghost, but these days there's all kinds of crazy names for bands," Jerry said. "Nirvana was at the King Center two days ago. Kurt is probably still in town if you want to go hang around outside his house. Some folks do that."

Hank caught an image of a body holding a shotgun. He wasn't sure where he remembered it from, but he shook it off. "No, I'm not the stalking type."

Jerry laughed. "Fair enough. Soundgarden is finishing up their shows with Neil Young in New York. Pearl Jam will be back in December, according to what I have here. They're in Canada right now. If you can stay until September 1st, the Screaming Trees, Spin Doctors, and Soul Asylum will be in Quincy."

"Sounds like I ported the wrong day for a show."

Jerry laughed again. It sounded practiced. "Maybe

so, sailor. Three Dog Night was supposed to play in three days on the eleventh, but they canceled for some Family Channel thing on the East Coast. If you're a time traveler or have access to a teleporter, you could catch a show from one of those bands. You can probably get all the way to the Three Dog show in the three days, if you were so inclined, I suppose."

"If that's where I'm supposed to be in three days, maybe I will. Thanks anyway, Jerry. What about sports? The Mariners or the Seahawks maybe?"

Jerry shuffled and then shrugged. "Mariners are away in Texas, but will play Kansas City at home on the 13th. The Seahawks season doesn't start until September 5th, and the first home game is on the twelfth against the Chargers."

"Maybe I'll just stroll around looking for clues to my destiny."

Jerry nodded and said, "Don't wander down I-90, if you can help it. They haven't finished the Lacy V Murrow bridge, so traffic is snarled that way. I-90 won't connect coast to coast again until next month."

"I'll adventure north and south then."

Jerry still turned pages. "You wouldn't happen to be a fan of The Neon Pickle Experience, are you?"

"Excuse me, Jerry?"

Jerry laughed. This time it seemed more real and unforced. "They are playing at the Pine Room on Broadway tonight. They're supposed to be good. Might be opening for Blind Melon in Spokane on the eleventh."

"I might do that, depending on how the day works out."

Jerry scribbled a map and directions on a pad of paper with the Silver Cloud Hotel letterhead. He finished by tearing the page off and folding it for Hank. "The Pine Room is marked Eleven Eleven with the address written out on the corner of the building in letters instead of numbers. Big silver letters: The Pine Room Eleven Eleven. If you get to a bar called The Rusty Nail, you've gone too far."

"Jerry Pine, are you related to the owners of the Pine Room?"

"No relation. Just coincidence."

I find few things are as coincidental as we think from my point of view, Jerry, Hank thought. *Anything could be a clue even though most things aren't.*

"Got it. Thank you, Jerry Pine, not of the Pine Room Broadway Pines." Hank pocketed the note and left the hotel. He never went back. He spent the day wandering and sitting. Then, he wandered some more.

As the sun dipped behind the world, he watched a grocer haul burlap bags of Idaho potatoes back inside for closing. *No local organic Seattle potatoes, I guess.* A guy on the corner strummed a guitar and sang a jangy folk song, "Where did you sleep last night?"

"Good question," Hank said to no one. A better question was where he was supposed to sleep tonight, and where he was supposed to port after that.

As with most problems, he decided to find somewhere to get a drink to think it out, or to not think about it at all, depending on how the night went.

The dirty street performer growled out the chorus again. "In the pines … in the pines … where sun don't ever shine … I will shiver the whole night through …"

Hank thought for a moment and pulled out the folded page from Jerry. The Neon Pickle Experience might be the only band in town, and the Pine Room was just as good a place as any to get a drink, he supposed. He made his way toward the bars on the strip they called Broadway in Seattle in 1993 and found Eleven Eleven written in letters and not numbers. He started drinking shortly after they opened and was buzzed by the time the flannel-clad ruffians of the Neon Pickles took the stage. They were too loud and played mostly other people's songs, but not as well. *No wonder they're the only ones still in town.*

They played a couple original songs toward the end, and the crowd started breaking apart. The tunes weren't terrible, but Hank had been to the future, and vintage The Neon Pickle Experience shirts were not the rage in any time he had visited. One was a song that wanted to be a ballad, but couldn't escape the Pickles' too heavy dissonant guitars. That one was "Cabin in the Cotton." They followed it by playing "Red Haired Angel on the Lake." It was repetitive and too long.

As Hank paid and prepared to leave, he realized he hadn't figured out where he was going next. He needed to stay somewhere. The Silver Cloud Hotel had looked too nice to take cash. It was 1993, so that was the borderline of when being a man with no name and no history started getting difficult.

The lead singer said, "Our last song is from a brother named Lead Belly. Blues man from the 40's. Doesn't get enough credit for being a genius. Where did you sleep last night?"

Hank paused at the door and turned around. "In the pines … In the pines …"

He had been ignoring clues all day. *Pines … Eleven … Three Dog Night … Three days from the eleventh? … Anything else? It could be something or nothing.* The same jangy tune from the 1940's played twice in 1993 Seattle couldn't be just nothing, could it? The dirty dude on the corner next to the Idaho potato bags played it better.

Hank scanned the room. He saw a guy with stringy blond hair and chilling blue eyes sitting in the corner. He and Hank seemed to be the only ones really listening to the song. The guy looked familiar. Hank stared a moment longer, but then just walked outside.

He backtracked toward the end of the Broadway bars. He thought he remembered passing a Motel 6 the way he had come.

"Eleven … three … six …" He repeated the numbers a few times. He tried to make something form in his brain around them, but they didn't even sound like real words anymore, after he mumbled them enough times.

A woman ran out of an alley and knocked over two guys. A third grabbed her arm and kept her from spilling into the street, too. She shook off his grip. "Get the fuck off of me."

As she ran away, the guy yelled after her, "Hey, you're bleeding, bitch."

Her red hair streamed behind her.

"Savannah! Savannah, wait." Hank ran after her as the guys picked themselves up out of the street.

She reached the corner ahead of him, dodging through the crowd better than he did.

"Savannah, it's me! Wait. Please."

She stopped and whirled around. Her eyes were wild and wide. She turned to go, and he was sure she would lose him on the next street. He was going to have to stop to throw up soon.

But she waited. She was bleeding from a deep slash down her shoulder and back through her shirt.

"What happened?" He coughed and wheezed the words more than he said them.

She turned on him, and he saw she had her satchel over her good shoulder with a long knife in that hand. He froze.

Savannah grabbed his wrist and dragged him along the road out of the lights outside the bars. Her hand shook on his, and eventually her grip fell away with her bad left arm dangling and dripping blood.

"Was it the dwarf?" Hank asked.

"That's not funny, Stranger."

"I'm not trying to be funny. And I'm Hank, by the way."

"Nice to meet you, Hank Stranger. Now help me get the hell out of here."

"Hank Smith. You need to get your shoulder patched up. You're bleeding a lot."

"I'd be bleeding a lot more, if I didn't keep moving."

"We need to get you to a hospital."

"There's no time for that, Stranger. I'll need you to help me do it. I have to be at the Pine Lake B&B in Pine, Idaho, Cabin 138, by the eleventh."

"I think I'm supposed to be there, too."

"Cool story, bro. Do you have a hotel room we can get to work in?"

"Um," Hank stopped in the street, but Savannah kept walking. He ran to catch up. "Wait. Let's figure this out. That cut is long and deep. You need stitches and probably antibiotics."

"How have you stayed alive this long, Stranger?"

Hank picked up his pace to get up to where he could see her profile. She was pale and sweaty. Blood had soaked the back of her shirt, he could tell even in the dark.

"What do you mean by that?"

"Haven't you figured out that antibiotics before the 2000's don't work on us? Or are you from an earlier time?"

"I don't know. Do you know what time you're from?"

"No, but I figured out old antibiotics work about as well as future money in the past. I figured that out the same day I discovered another jumper had a 'super long-term' storage unit deal near mine. Can't believe you use the same name for everything in every time. Do pre twenty-first century antibiotics work on you?"

"I … I don't know. I've managed to stay out of hospitals."

"We shouldn't break that streak now." She finally did stop and looked back the way they had come. Drops of blood marked the sidewalk behind them. He couldn't tell if she saw that or was looking for whoever had cut her.

Bloody breadcrumbs for whatever is chasing her.

They both spoke at the same time. "We need to get off the street."

Chapter 6

August 9th, 1993 - Seattle, Washington

The Motel 6 didn't have a room 138, but they didn't need to port anyway. In room 112's bathroom, Savannah washed the deep cut on her shoulder, her shirt ruined. The door was open and Hank watched from the other room.

"You keep calling me stranger," Hank said.

"You're a stranger to me. We haven't really met. Not like this."

"Not like this ... you mean actually having a conversation or meeting while you try unsuccessfully to stop the bleeding?" Hank paced. He wanted to help, but knew she needed a doctor. "I'm sure we can find a shady doctor who can patch you up for cash without any questions or cops."

"I'm not interested in a shady back alley butcher

ruining my arm," Savannah said.

She took off her bloody shirt, which made Hank look away. He turned from her to a cheap hotel painting of a train crossing a trestle above a street. All the details around the painting were dull and fuzzy.

Savannah laughed. "Such a gentleman." She ripped the fabric into strips. "I think I can get it to stop bleeding."

"What if you can't?"

"Then I die." She sighed. "Got anything to eat? I was trying to sneak out of a bar tab and those men decided I needed to pay. I haven't eaten in a couple of days." Savannah glanced at Hank and smiled. "Or years. It's so hard to figure out."

"I don't have anything, but I have some cash that will work. I can order a pizza. Do they deliver in 1993, or do I need to go pick it up?" Hank was still trying to get his facts straight about each timeframe, but porting through over a hundred years of time made figuring it all out slow.

"You can get it delivered. I remember ordering from Domino's Pizza in the late seventies. The pizza was actually better than today, I think. This hour though, I don't know." Savannah wrapped her arm and shoulder in the makeshift bandages.

"Better than today? You mean 1993 or another year?" Hank laughed at his lame joke.

Savannah did not. "I mean any year. 1970's pizza was just better. Same with fast food burgers. They didn't have all the GMOs and unnatural hormones we feed our plants and animals today. By today, I mean 1993, but pretty much anything the last few years and in the future."

Hank used the phone in the room to call 411 and get the number to a pizza place, which ended up being some 24 hour place with a name he'd never be able to spell or find in a phonebook himself. "What do you want on your pizza?"

"Pepperoni. See if they have Coke products, too. I doubt they've invented cheesy bread yet, though." Savannah laughed. "Mention it to them. Maybe it will be the push they need to create it."

"I don't want to change history," Hank said.

Savannah laughed again. "Didn't you ever see the *Star Trek* movie where they give that guy the formula to create the metal they'd need to repair their ship?"

"I'm more of a *Star Wars* fan, although discovering them after everyone knew about Vader and Luke being related spoiled it for me."

Savannah groaned. "I haven't seen them yet. Thanks for spoiling it. Jerk."

"Sorry." Hank, red-faced, ordered the pizza.

"I was just kidding," Savannah said, when he hung up.

"You don't want pepperoni pizza?"

Blood seeped through the fabric. "No, I *so* want pizza. I mean about *Star Wars*. I saw it, but got to see the first one in 1977 at a drive-in. Before I knew about the rest. Of course, I rented the next ones in the future. I think I saw all of them, even the spinoffs and cartoons. All the streaming stuff after Disney took it over."

Hank didn't understand every reference she made. "So you're a big fan?"

"I'm a fan of killing time. On a couple of ports lately I've had a lot of time on my hands. Sometimes weeks between jumps. Once I was trapped in Montreal for nine months. It snowed a lot, but I learned French." Savannah sat down on the bed. "You're not getting lucky with me."

"Huh?" Hank felt himself blushing. He looked at the phone. At the wall. The shitty train painting. "I didn't think…"

"Lighten up. I'm teasing you again. I know we had to get one bed or it would look suspicious. I'm sure by now the police are looking for me. Do you ever worry about doing something wrong in one time and getting caught for it years later?"

"I try not to do anything stupid. No offense." Hank said. He sat down on the chair at the desk. "I'm very smart about not leaving my footprint anywhere, if I can help it. I'm scared I'll change something, and it will affect a future me or the future of mankind."

Savannah snickered. "I'm sure that's what happened when you mentioned cheesy bread tonight."

"I didn't mention it," Hank said.

She shook her head. "You're really lame. I'm sure people have told you that before."

Hank looked away. She was messing with him, and he suspected she wasn't doing it to be mean, but it still hurt. She was smiling and trying to see what buttons to push, learn more about him. While he'd done it many times to many people in many different years, it still stung.

Savannah was the first person who could actually understand what he was going through, where he'd been and where he might be headed.

"What if I told you I didn't want you coming with me to Idaho?" Savannah asked. She'd stopped smiling.

Hank snapped his neck to look at her again. " No. Come on. By my best guess and journals, I've been porting for at least ten years. It's hard to give an exact time, of course. The days flow in an order but not the year. I can go to sleep in Chicago and wake the next day in Chicago. My position in the world doesn't change. The clock itself moves at the same second by second rate no matter where I am. And yet… the year is different. Everything around me is either older or younger. I could be in Chicago and meet an old man, retired and bent over using a cane, taking his time to go to the corner store to buy a paper. The next day this man is a child, running down the same block to the same newspaper stand to buy a paper for his grandfather."

"I know. I do the same thing," she said.

Hank snapped his fingers. "Exactly. You understand what I just said. What the meaning is. I didn't have to explain it to you because you're in the same boat."

"Your point, stranger?"

"My point is we're not strangers. I have no real memories of a former life, before I started porting. Do you?"

Savannah shook her head slowly.

"We could be brother and sister."

"Doubtful," she said. "We don't look alike."

"Maybe we were married? We're about the same age."

Savannah snorted. "What age is that? How old am I in 1993? What if I haven't even been born yet? What if I'm already long dead?"

"There's a reason we're both involved, and we finally met." Hank was out of the chair now and pacing. "We just need to figure out why."

"I have a question for you. Maybe two." Savannah stood and wandered the room as well. "What if we both go to Idaho and then find room 138 and lie down in the same bed together… and I wake up in 1834 and you're in 2034?"

Hank stopped pacing. "Why did you choose 2034 as a year?"

Savannah shrugged. "I'm not sure."

"What's the furthest year you've ever gone?"

She shook her head and went to her satchel, pulling out a thick notebook, the corners dog-eared. She began flipping through pages, and Hank could see tiny writing on each line that had not been in there when he had her satchel. He wished it had been.

"I keep notebooks, but with a lot more detail in them," Hank said. "Can I read yours?"

"No, you can't. I used to, but it got tedious. I used to study them for a pattern. Try to find a city or year I'd gone back to more than twice. I never found it at all." Savannah pointed at a sheet. "I was in Milwaukee in the summer of 2034." She turned a few more pages. "Hartford in December 2034. New Year's Eve San Francisco same year."

Hank sighed. "I know there was talk of war when I was in 2034, but I ignored it. I'd been to many years where the talk was about World War II or Vietnam or Desert Storm. Again, for me it was about leaving as little footprint as possible and not changing anything in the world."

"I keep thinking I'll buy a book listing all the Super Bowl winners and then place a bet, depending on where I am, but the problem is I never get back to that year to collect. The only way to do it is know the dates and whatever year you land in late January or early February you get to Vegas and plunk down a few grand and then not have to worry about money again," Savannah said.

"Yeah, I tried it in the 80s." Hank shook his head. "What if you won it this year? You'll get money that's no good in any previous year. Maybe the last few with circulation, but definitely nothing from, say, twenty years ago. Plus they change the way bills are printed a few times. I have a lot of mixed bills I can't even use. Some printed in 2034 I can only use that year."

"Which brings us back to worrying about what happens in 2034."

Hank had hoped she'd have all the answers. Unfortunately, this conversation led to having even more questions on both sides. While Savannah had figured a few more things out than Hank, she was still in the dark as to the how and why.

"In your note, you mentioned other porters… jumpers. I always thought I was unique, up until I first saw you." Hank was exhausted and not just physically. This conversation was getting to him, frustrating, and a part of him wanted to stop it. Act like it was any other night in a hotel and pizza was coming. Watch a ballgame or a sitcom. Maybe at this hour, an infomercial. Talk about the weather.

When Savannah didn't answer right away, he turned to her and frowned.

She was crying, a tear running down her cheek as she covered her eyes.

Hank went to her, but she held him at arm's length.

"I don't want to talk about it tonight," she said and opened her eyes, wiping tears with her sleeve. She chuckled. "I'm such a girl sometimes. Sorry. I lost someone I knew. Another one of us."

He knew that much from the note. Hank wanted to drill her for information, but knew she'd clam up. Why hadn't she led with that? "I'm here if you want to talk about it. At least I'm someone else who would understand."

"True."

There was a knock at the door and pizza arrived, which helped break the tension in the room.

"I think I was in Idaho once or twice, but usually it was to drive through to get to somewhere else," Hank said between bites of pizza. Despite all of his travels, he didn't think he could find Idaho on a map. It was one of those in-between places.

"When I started keeping track, I used a notebook, but also set up an online private site as well," Savannah said. She'd washed her face once the pizza guy had left and didn't look like she'd been crying. "It's crashed a couple of times, though. I also made the mistake of setting it up in 2009, so it doesn't exist before that year."

"You could make a copy on a thumb drive and go in earlier."

"That doesn't work on earlier computers." She shrugged. "Finding ways to transfer formats seems like a lot of work, and when I went back to add a few more ports in, I realized some of them I didn't even remember."

Hank was nodding. "I write them down in notebooks. Quite a few are gone from my memory, too. It's like I can remember vivid details from the last two dozen, but according to the books, I've done this hundreds of times. I've been all over the country." He thought of a question. "Have you gone out of North America?"

Savannah shook her head. "Definitely not that I can remember and not according to my records, but they're incomplete. I imagine so are yours."

"We could compare books," he said.

"Maybe." She shrugged it off this time instead of just saying no.

Hank had been eating and when Savannah stopped at two pieces he finished the pizza. Now he was sleepy. "Can you do me a favor? Please don't leave me."

Savannah smiled. "It was an option until we shared pizza. I didn't want to involve you."

"I am definitely involved. I feel like we weren't supposed to have met."

She nodded. "I understand that. Can we promise one another something?"

"Sure."

"No lies between us. No secrets. I feel like maybe we're not supposed to be aligned as well. This could be a really good thing." Savannah cleaned up the pizza scraps and box

Hank looked at her satchel and thought about her notebook. *No lies? No secrets?*

She said, "But I'm asking you another thing: tomorrow we talk about nothing important."

"Works for me." He pulled his eyes away from the bag. "I could use a break."

Savannah turned and stared at Hank, but she was smiling. "I'm serious. We find an amusement park or go to a movie. Have dinner. Only when we're headed to Pine Idaho, which is about nine hours away, do we get back to being miserable and feeling trapped chasing after something we might never get our hands on."

Chapter 7

August 11th 1993 - Pine, Idaho

Hank spoke as he stepped out of the passenger's side, in front of the lodge and main office. "So, is the dwarf real or is he not? I mean like a real human real."

Her voice came muffled from inside the car as she wrestled with the stubborn lock. "Jesus Christ, how many times do you need me to retell it? It's been nine hours of this."

Hank chewed the inside of his mouth. She had finally relented on letting him see her notebook, but it really didn't tell him anything. She passed on seeing his journals.

He said, "We played the license plate game for a while, too."

"Not better." She slammed the driver's door with the sound of a vault door.

"So, Alice was killed by him, and you don't know for certain if either one was a porter or not? Not for sure? You think Alice was, but you're not positive?"

Savannah took a deep breath and let it out as they approached the steps of the lodge. The porch of the place overlooked the lake in the distance. A long row of wooden rocking chairs lined the porch, all empty.

They both adjusted their satchels with the cryptic buttons facing out. She said, "Alice wasn't in her right mind any time I met her, but she ranted about slipstream and unanchored consciousness and quantum entanglement. She was a teenager when I met her in 2012 in Red Rock, Texas. She was a grown woman, when I met her, if it was the same person, in 1980 Los Angeles. The Alice I met in 1926 was elderly and missing an eye. That's when she was killed. I never saw her jump. She acted like she remembered me each time, but never remembered my name. I can't imagine her having it together enough to find and decipher clues. I tried to protect her, and I couldn't. That's it."

Hank said, "In the note, you said you thought she was a porter … or a jumper."

She put her hand on the handle to the lodge's front door and paused. She didn't respond to him.

Hank cleared his throat and said, "Killed by the same dwarf you saw in 2034 in December?"

"Yes, if he actually was the same one, and I'm not dreaming my entire life, including this stupid conversation. Yes. He chased me then and chased Alice until she was hit by a truck in 1926. Can this wait until we secure the cabin for our next jump?"

"Yes."

She opened the door, and they walked in together. Savannah leaned on the counter for the front desk with her satchel flipped behind her back. Hank stood behind her, holding the strap in both hands. He squeezed the 138 button inside his palm.

A man with a thick white beard and mustache smiled as he approached Savannah from his side of the desk. "Welcome. Welcome. You two are either mighty lost or accidentally found the most beautiful vacation spot on Earth."

"I think we're in the right place," she said with a giggle. Her voice took on a lilting, girly tone that made Hank's skin crawl for some reason. "We wanted to see which cabins you still had available."

The man turned to a chart on the wall which included a map of the lake and a road twisting around it. He pointed inside the diagram of the lodge. "We have rooms here which include complimentary breakfast and meals for purchase in the afternoon and evening. If you two want to remain undisturbed, we have a few cabins still available for rent."

"Which cabins?" Savannah asked.

He hummed and then pointed. "Here, here, and, ugh, this one. You have to follow this road out to get to 144. You can still see the lake from the hill though. You have to drive in to get meals here, but the cabins have kitchens and full facilities."

"What about that one there?"

Hank didn't have to look to see where she was pointing.

"Which one?"

She leaned over the desk farther. "That one. Top center."

He found the spot. "No, that one's rented to a honeymooning couple all week. These others are just as fine, though."

"We kind of had our heart set on that one," Hank chimed in.

"Did you?" The man eyed Hank, and his smile faded underneath the bushy mustache. "138 was your heart's desire?"

"144 will be fine," Savannah said. "Can we do a cash deposit for one night or how does that work?"

"We just drove past 138, and it looked so nice, you know? Is there anything that can be done?" Hank felt he needed to interject. He didn't like the way the guy was sizing them up now.

"Yeah, lots can be done. Lots of things are done all the time. 138 is the one? Is that it?"

Savannah put her hand on Hank's chest and faced him with eyes wide and piercing. Her satchel swung around to her side, and he let go of the strap to his bag. She said, "No, Honey, 144 will work fine. Okay?"

Hank nodded, but the man grabbed Savannah's bag by the strap and jerked her backward. "Let me see that."

Hank lifted his fists, but she twisted the man's wrist and slammed his forearm into the counter, forcing him to let go. Her girly voice was gone. "Hands, creep."

"I've never seen two of you at once." His face grew red, either from anger or the impact, and he balled his fists on the counter. He was angry, but seemed unhurt. "What the hell is it with this game? Do you guys just screw with me every couple years, or is this going on all over the country?"

Savannah stepped back from the desk toward the door. "What are you talking about?"

He pointed back and forth between them. "138. Right there on your man purses. Are you just breaking in there to screw? Is there some weird cult thing going on? Vandalism? Tell me."

"Other people have come here looking for room 138?" Hank asked.

The man grabbed a heavy green rotary phone and slammed it down on the counter, making the bell inside it chime in an incomplete tone. "Before I call the cops to have you two run off for trespassing, just tell me, is it as simple as changing the cabin number? I almost did that after the last woman broke into the place in '89. I'll definitely do it now. When you write to your sick friends from jail, tell them there is no 138 up here anymore."

"Who were they?" Hank took a step forward. "What were the names of the others before us?"

The man lifted the receiver and dialed zero.

Savannah grabbed Hank's arm and dragged him out of the lodge.

Hank asked her, "Have you been here before? In 1989 or earlier?"

"No, dummy. Keep going." She opened the car door and started the engine before Hank got in.

As he closed his door, he said, "I always wondered if hotels would start to catch on to stuff getting stolen from room 138 all the time. You know? Like at the chains where maybe I had done it more than once in multiple cities? But the incidents were decades apart. But it happened here in Nowhere, Idaho."

They pulled away from the lodge and circled the lake road toward the north.

"138 is the other way," he said.

A radio announcer finished a report on Tropical Storm Bret crossing Nicaragua where it was gaining strength again in the Pacific, and then he started on Pope John Paul II's coming visit to the U.S. She turned off the radio.

"I know. But I don't want to park a stolen car in front of the place while we wait for the couple to leave the cabin for dinner."

"Stolen?" He looked around the interior like he expected to see it was bugged by the CIA. "You said you bought it off a used car lot."

"Bought. Borrowed. Claimed. Stolen. They probably haven't noticed yet, and if they did, the BOLO reports aren't computerized yet and sure aren't faxed to places like Pine, Idaho. Still, we got no papers on it, if the police stop us because Mountain Man Jim called them down on us."

"Savannah." He shook his head and stared out the window for a moment. "This kind of thing can have a big impact on history. What if ..."

She laughed. "What if what, Doctor? If this used car isn't in the right place in 1993, then they don't cure cancer in 2050?"

"They cured cancer in 2050?"

"I don't know. We haven't been past New Year's 2034. I'm just saying. What do you think will change?"

"You know ... I don't know. The Butterfly Effect, right?"

"This car will affect the butterflies?"

Hank sighed. "No. The Butterfly Effect. A butterfly flaps its wings in Africa. It kicks up dust. A gazelle sneezes. The herd runs. The wind builds and there is a rainstorm in America." He motioned at the radio. "Tropical Storm Bret becomes a hurricane. Someone dies in a car crash who should have lived. The Pope's plane crashes. You know. Like that."

"I understand Chaos Theory, but..." Savannah shook her head as she stared forward and drove. "Do you believe rain is caused by stampeding animals, Hank?"

"No, but, I mean, all events work together. They are intertwined in a web. You can't pull at just one string."

"I get the theory; I just don't buy it, not when it

comes to time travel. I've thought about this a lot. It just doesn't add up to me that..." She paused to sigh. "Okay, Hank Smith, riddle me this. If I wanted to make it rain and I had all the money in the world, is there anything I could do to make it rain? Could I? This week? Could I control the rain in a year? Has anyone in all of human history ever figured out how to change the weather?"

"What's your point?"

She slapped one hand against the steering wheel. "That's not how rain is made. Butterflies don't change anything. If this car is a butterfly in an unknowable Chaos Theory equation across all of time and space, it won't change the weather or history."

"It's a metaphor. Or an analogy. I don't know. It means we can cause changes by the things we do everywhere we port. We shouldn't have more of an impact than we have to."

"Well, Hank, we encountered fewer people this way than we would buying bus tickets and taking taxis, right? Let's say I made someone late by buying the last bus ticket, but probably not because they would just buy the next one. She wasn't meant to meet anyone on that bus because she wasn't going to talk to anyone. Let's say I cut someone off in traffic. They got caught by the lights and stayed on the road later. Does that mean they die in a fiery accident? No, because when the dude sees a car stop in front of him, he'll just put on his brakes like every other time, and he won't have an accident."

"If he's late for dinner, his wife might be mad. She

could divorce him," Hank said. "Men are more likely to die sooner after divorce, statistically."

"If she's going to divorce him, it will be for other stuff before and after that." Savannah said. "The world isn't as fragile as butterfly wings, no matter how cool that sounds to armchair philosophers who enjoy time travel movies. Most of what we do won't change anything. What we do change, won't mean much. Could everything we do in all our jumps through time combined buy the Earth one more day? We're not that important, Hank, I promise."

She pulled off the road and backed the hulk of a car as far into the thicket as she could get. Hank scraped his door and his cheek getting out. They followed through the woods off the road and came up behind cabin 138.

There was a light on inside. A figure passed a window. They stayed behind the trees and sat down on the ground to wait.

"How long should we wait?" Hank said.

"They'll leave soon. If they've been at it all day, they'll be hungry, and she'll be looking for an excuse to give it a rest."

"What if they decide to cook dinner for themselves?"

"I'm guessing she doesn't know how, and they didn't bring enough groceries."

Hank waited a while longer. "What if they don't leave though? We're cutting this a little close."

"We'll break out the back window, chase them out, lock ourselves in, and try to jump before the cops can break in."

"That might change history," Hank said.

Savannah sniffed and shook her head. "Maybe."

"You think they're watching the cabin, waiting for us? The police, I mean."

"Hank, I'm not sure Pine PD has the manpower to stakeout a cabin based on some guy calling and complaining that two people came to rent a cabin that was already rented, you know? If he sells it the way he told us, it's going to sound like conspiracy theory nonsense."

"Yeah, I guess."

"You didn't play it very cool back there, at all. We could have rented another cabin or just walked away, and we'd be fine right now. You blew it, Mr. Small Footprint."

"We wouldn't have learned about others like us coming to port here though."

"So, great work, Hank Sherlock."

"His last name was Holmes."

"*His last name was Holmes,*" she repeated in a high, snotty voice. "Nerd."

"And playing it cool? You slammed his hand against the counter."

"Dudes need to learn to keep their hands to themselves."

The honeymoon couple did leave, and then drove away from the lodge toward the main road.

"Where do you think they're going?" Hank said, as

they approached the backdoor of the cabin.

With her satchel over her elbow, she shattered the back glass and unlocked the door. "Maybe the food at the lodge sucks."

The glass crunched under their feet as they walked inside. In the bedroom, the comforter was on the floor at the end of the bed, and a torn pair of lacy underwear hung on a doorknob. The sheets were balled up and looked damp. A smell like chlorine, sweat, and air freshener swilled through the bedroom.

Savannah covered her nose. "You go ahead. I think I'll stay here and just let my atoms scatter to the stars when I miss the jump."

Hank tossed the comforter over the top of the ruffled sheets. "Come on. Let's get it over with."

"Stay on your side and hands to yourself."

"Yeah, I don't want my wrist smashed." Hank rolled his eyes and laid down on the bed, clutching his satchel.

As she lay next to him, she said, "I don't know if I can fall asleep with you in here. It feels weird."

"You will. I laid down late once or twice and the port knocked me out when I wouldn't fall asleep on my own."

"That sounds unpleasant."

"It'll be fine." He swallowed a couple times as he stared up at the ceiling. "Try to find me."

"Found you. You're right there. Now, shut up."

"No, I mean, if we don't port to the same place this

time, keep an eye out for me. The more often we meet up, the sooner we may figure this all out."

"Sure thing, Holmes Hank. Now, shut the trap, and go to sleep."

"I'm serious, Savannah."

"I'm serious, too. Shut up, already. If we see each other, we'll team up again. We may not have power over it, but let's play the quiet game until we jump."

Spots showed up in his vision, and light blasted out at him from every surface. He felt himself going under.

Her voice echoed through his head, when she said, "Oh, God, what's happening?"

"It'll be okay. You'll port soon and everything …"

Chapter 8

August 12th 2016 - Baton Rouge, Louisiana

Hank faded back into awareness standing in the corner of a poorly lit hotel room.

He waited for the motion in the room to end as the occupants left. The door hung open and wavered by a few inches back and forth. The hallway was dark, too.

He realized the motion in the room was an upholstered chair and a lamp floating in brown water which had risen almost above the top of the mattress. A potted plant drifted by in the hallway.

Hank stumbled forward and became solid and present just in time to feel cold and wet up to his crotch. He lifted his satchel on top of his shoulder, away from the water. An information booklet for La Quinta Inn floated past him.

He waded to the window and saw the water in the back parking lot had risen above the door handles of the cars. It was morning, but overcast.

Savannah was nowhere around. No one was anywhere around except him.

For a moment, he was filled with fear. Not just fear, but full terror. He pictured water surging up over him as he screamed for God to save him. It was there for an intense moment, and then it was gone. His heart still beat rapidly, but the vision was gone.

Was that a memory? It wasn't a pleasant one.

Real or not, he had an actual flood to deal with here and now.

"It's a shame 138 is on the first floor, La Quinta." The water was cold, but the room had to be 100 degrees with 100% humidity. A flood. "Well, this is new."

Hank waded through the water and into the hallway, which smelled of mold and sewage. He could hear the soft drizzle of rain down the hall, where the exit door used to be. It had been yanked off its hinges and was twisted against the wall.

Someone had carved into the wall with jagged letters: MR. TRAIN IS GOD.

"Don't do drugs, kids," Hank muttered to himself.

Water lapped outside, and Hank could see a few cars that weren't going anywhere soon, if ever.

Had it rained so hard the ground was saturated and the hotel area was flooded? Hank instinctively knew it was something bigger. A river had grown past its banks due to the storm, and he'd be walking for miles to escape it.

Knowing he needed to leave the hotel, but also knowing he'd be soaked, Hank looked for something to keep him dry. Maybe a jacket or an umbrella, although it sounded like there was a strong wind outside.

The couple who'd recently vacated the room … Hank stopped. There'd been no one in this room for hours. Maybe a couple of days. Something was off. He always ended up in a room 138 with someone just leaving the room, and mostly leaving something of value behind.

Hank went back into the room and searched the top drawers, which were the only ones not soaked yet. He found a dog-eared Bible in the first drawer and a bundle of clothing in the second.

When Hank lifted the clothes a wad of cash in a sealed plastic bag as well as a .22 shook loose. He stared at the items. While he'd been lucky enough in the past to find money and the occasional weapon, this somehow felt wrong, as if the pair of items had been left for him to find. Unless this storm and water surge had come unexpectedly, he assumed whoever was in this room wouldn't have left anything of real value.

Hank, on a hunch, went to the closet and opened it. Empty. The drawers already in water yielded nothing but a drawer full of water.

Whoever had been staying in the room was long gone.

What Hank had found in the drawer wasn't left behind. It was placed there. He looked closer at the clothes: two pairs of new socks, a pair of men's underwear in his size, a black t-shirt with *Max's Kansas City* written in script across the front, also in his size, and a Kansas City Royals baseball cap with *Kevin McCarthy* written inside the brim.

He stuffed the items in his satchel along with the money and weapon and left the hotel by the broken side door, stepping out into rain, wind in his face, and water lapping to his crotch.

The electricity was out, and he didn't see anyone around, not even rescue personnel. He assumed everyone had been smart enough to evacuate hours or days ago, knowing the impending storm was about to hit.

Was this a hurricane? Hank didn't think so. Despite the winds, it was more flooding than anything else. Maybe a dam had broken, although he was in Baton Rouge. He didn't think he was near the water like New Orleans.

For all he knew, he still didn't know enough. Everywhere he went he felt like he was missing something vitally important. He knew random, weird facts about places, but never enough to feel like he was born or raised in a certain city or town.

He slowly waded past a billboard that read: Clocksmith's On Main – Fixing time one piece at a time.

Hank rolled his eyes and kept going at a labored pace. Was that supposed to be a clue or a taunt?

Ask Mr. Train to part these waters for me since he's God.

His thoughts drifted around in his wet misery.

Once he found somewhere that felt like home, would he stay? He didn't think so. What if he was actually born in 1897 or 2027? Finding his birthplace or where he grew up in 2016 wasn't going to help. He'd either be long gone or waiting to be born.

Hank thought about Marty McFly and meeting his parents in *Back To The Future* and smiled. For obvious reasons he enjoyed the series, even the last one, which most folks thought was pushing it a bit.

Time travel movies, TV shows, and books were fun to enjoy, but they didn't help with what Hank was going through. Savannah had been the first real help he'd ever known, as far as his limited memory could prove, and now she was off on another tangent and time.

Hank wondered if she was thinking about him.

The rain was still steady and the wind gusted, driving the rain into Hank's face and making him miserable.

Hank was soaked by the time he walked a couple of miles, but the ground slowly rose and he was now walking through puddles and not knee-deep water. The runoff from higher ground was filling the natural basin he was walking in, even though the ground around him looked relatively flat. Even a few inches dipping would fill up quickly and make it slow going.

He paused to assess the pain he was in. It wasn't just the ache and discomfort of being wet and dirty. A couple spots hurt so bad he thought he might really be injured. He lifted his shirt to see a fresh bruise on his belly and scratches everywhere. Looking around for traffic and then feeling foolish for doing so, he unbuckled his pants and checked his legs. More bruises and scratches covered him there. It must have been from all the debris in the flood waters.

"The La Quinta Inn brochure didn't say anything about this," he said. Pulling his soggy pants back up bothered him more than all the scratches and bruises.

He felt wet to the point that he couldn't imagine ever being dry again. No telling what diseases he'd exposed himself to in that muck, and with all these scratches. At least post 2000 antibiotics would be available … along with a few more antibiotic resistant strains of nastiness.

The rain had slowed to a mist, but it was getting dark. The wind had dulled, but it still whispered in his ears, giving him a headache.

For now he was alone on the road.

Up ahead he saw lights. Someone still had electricity. As he got closer, he saw it was a truckstop, and the lot was full. This was the closest spot he'd been to with lights, and he hoped he'd found food.

He wasn't the only one with the same idea.

Every parking space was taken, not only with big rigs, but cars. People paced back and forth between the cars and the building. Hank could see there was, indeed, a restaurant, and by the looks of the long line snaking out of it, they had food.

Despite the steady rain, he didn't hear much complaining in line as everyone waited for a turn and a hot meal. Hank initially thought getting in line because he was hungry and thirsty, but decided to get changed first.

Even if he'd need to go back into the rain at some point, it would be nice to be dry for an hour or so. He got in a smaller line, this one for the men's room, and squeezed into a stall. He changed his socks and underwear and put on the t-shirt and baseball cap, stuffing his wet clothes into his bag and hoping it wouldn't ruin anything inside. The bruises had begun to set in wide and dark across his skin all over.

Then it was time to get food. He only had a few dollars on him he was willing to part with. Hank decided fries and a drink would be enough, since he had no idea how far he'd need to travel and didn't want to pull out a bag of dry money in front of anyone. He supposed he should have checked his money situation while he was changing.

Another missed opportunity. Water under the bridge and through the La Quinta.

Hank kept to himself, but also kept an eye on his surroundings and everyone around him.

Since meeting Savannah and finding out he wasn't alone he felt… not as special? Hank didn't think that was the right word for it. He now knew there was something bigger in motion here, and he felt… insignificant.

That was the right word.

Paranoia … Time travel psychosis …

Even though he'd gone through his life (well, what

he could remember of it) feeling like he was special and making a significant difference in the world, even though it was still a mystery how he was doing it, he knew it had been a lie, a facade.

Others across time struggled with the mysteries of Room 138 as well. Gone was his sense of being unique. There might be dozens of porters like him and Savannah out there.

Hank looked around at the crowd. How many others were in this very truck stop, trying to get to their next room 138, just trying to survive like he was?

There was a mural of a multi-colored spiral on the wall that made him dizzy and added to his headache. He found somewhere else to look.

Hank shook his head and stuffed a few fries in his mouth as soon as he sat in a booth at the far end of the main room. He needed to calm down and not get upset. He'd been in spots like this before, with a couple of clues and no real sense of urgency to make a quick port.

Enjoy a very wet Baton Rouge, and next time I'm in town, it will be sunny, and this truck stop might be a densely wooded area with a horse and carriage on a muddy road, Hank thought.

"Mind if I join you? Seating is at a premium tonight."

Hank looked up to see a bald man with an eyepatch and a crooked smile. His clothes were damp, and it smelled like he'd just bathed in whatever body spray they sold in the trucker bathroom. He looked friendly enough.

"Sure." Hank was finishing up his fries and drink and would be moving on soon anyway.

"Thanks. You a local?"

Hank, trying to be nice, shook his head.

The man put his own satchel on the seat next to him and Hank stared at it.

The man patted the bag. "Everything I own is inside. Not much at all." He seemed to notice Hank's satchel. "Ha. I see you're traveling light as well. I hope you got your important documents out of the house." He patted it again before opening the top. "I need to send a few emails. I hope the wi-fi is working. On normal days this place is spotty."

Hank smiled, but was wary. Even though the man's satchel was different from the one he carried or Savannah had, maybe he'd switched his out to throw another porter off or people like the man renting the cabins in Pine who were clued into the 138s.

The man was busy with a laptop. He glanced at the fries on the table.

Hank pushed the rest over to him.

"No. I couldn't. I appreciate it, but I'll be fine. I just need to find somewhere with a working bank machine. The one here is out."

"I'm done with them. Please. I insist," Hank said. He folded his hands on the table. "Besides, maybe we could make a trade for them."

The man pursed his lips. "I'm not into men."

Hank laughed. "Neither am I. I mean, since your computer is working, maybe you can look up a couple of things for me."

"Like what?" His one eye squinted. "You need a hotel or a phone number?"

Hank smiled. "I need help with the name of a baseball player."

"I'm Finn." He extended a hand.

Hank shook it. "Larry."

The guy could be just another traveler or a local washed out of his home, but Hank was taking no chances. A few days ago, he wouldn't have thought anything more than wanting to know why he was wearing an eyepatch and how to broach the subject.

Now Hank saw evil porters and friends of the dwarf in every face, knowing how ridiculous it was. He'd always been careful, but for the reasons he gave Savannah: he was afraid to leave a carbon footprint in another time and change the course of history. Carbon wasn't the right word. Maybe he meant temporal footprint, whether Savannah believed in the Butterfly Effect or not.

"A baseball player, huh?" Finn hesitated, but took the fries from Hank. "Is he a friend of yours?" He pointed at Hank's Royals baseball cap. "You're a distance from K.C. and most of the main roads are flooded out. You need to send him an email?"

Hank shook his head. "Nothing as exciting as that. A friend of mine likes to give me cryptic messages so

I can figure out where she'll head to next." He studied Finn's face to see if the man had any recognition about porting, or if he knew Hank was lying.

Either Finn was excellent at poker or he was just a traveler with an eyepatch and a smile.

Finn licked his fingers as he ate the fries and wiped his hand on his damp pants. "What's his name?"

"Kevin McCarthy," Hank said, nearly taking off his cap to double-check, but deciding that would be too weird. He needed to play this cool.

Finn salted the remaining fries some more and then put down the shaker. "Someone stole our pepper."

"Do you put pepper on your fries?"

"No, but it's bad luck to have salt sitting on a table without pepper."

The people moved in and out of the building around him, as more and more found the safe haven of the truck stop. More people meant anyone looking for or following him would blend in with the crowds.

Finn typed away on his laptop and smiled. "Okay, what do you need to know about him?"

"I'm not sure. Is there a bio or his stats?"

Finn turned the laptop so they could both look at it.

Hank shrugged. Nothing was jumping out at him. Sometimes the clues were so obvious and he knew not to second-guess them.

"Anything? Is this a game you've been playing for a long time?" Finn asked.

"A couple of months. I'm thinking she's in Kansas

City."

Finn looked at Hank's shirt and back to the screen, putting up a finger. "Wait… is she usually this easy to figure out? You're wearing a Max's Kansas City shirt. Did she give it to you or is this a coincidence?"

Hank sighed. "She left it for me." He knew Savannah hadn't been the one to leave it. Whoever had stayed in that particular room 138 last had left it.

In your exact size and with a wad of cash? It wasn't a coincidence, Hank thought. There was something else going on. Something he needed to figure out.

And fast.

"Max's Kansas City was a club in New York City. It closed in the early 1980's. I saw a documentary about it not too long ago." Finn smiled. "I think your friend is in New York City."

Hank shook his head. It didn't feel right. Kansas City felt like it was the destination.

Finn clapped his hands. "In fact…" he pointed at the screen. "Your ballplayer was born in New York. That has to mean something, too."

Hank nodded slowly, trying to wrap his head around it.

He'd had clues like this in the past, but his gut had always told him which way to go, which path was right. He was definitely having another moment as Kansas City made more sense for whatever reason.

"Plus, I'm headed to drop off a load in New York City," Finn said. "You can come with me. Keep me company. As soon as I get out of Louisiana and find a bank, I'll pay you back for the fries, too. I know a great hole in the wall on I-10 in Jacksonville. They serve some great southern food."

Hank shook his head. "I need to get to Kansas City. Thanks for the offer."

"I think you're making a big mistake," Finn said.

Hank stood. Was Finn being a nice guy, or was he trying to confuse him? Then it hit Hank, another gut check: Finn was trying to send him in the wrong direction.

"Thanks. Good luck in New York City," Hank mumbled and ran.

He couldn't help but to look at that spiral on the wall on his way out. It screwed with his already boggled mind.

What do you see?

Hank looked away.

He was back outside, the rain heavy again. The parking lot was beginning to flood and more people were leaving now.

Hank asked around until he got a ride from a trucker headed to Missouri, thankful he hadn't been thrown off course.

His fear of going to the wrong room 138 and being trapped in one time, and not the time he was supposed to be in, drove him to assess each clue.

More than anything, he needed to keep trusting his gut.

Chapter 9

August 16, 2016 - Kansas City, Missouri

He made it to Kansas City with days to wander. Every sign seemed to have some hidden meaning. Every object a clue. Every woman or flash of red in the distance was Savannah, for just an instant. Every child on the street was the dangerous dwarf in Hank's peripheral, coming out to get him from fairy tales told by a woman disconnected from time, just like him.

He found a boutique hotel that was too expensive to stay in long term, but it had a room 138, and Hank felt edgy. He couldn't get the pieces to fit, and he couldn't find anything to pass the time or to settle his nerves.

The Raphael Hotel, Signature Series, overlooked Brush Creek in downtown Kansas City. A few blocks east was McCarthy Memorial Park. It was a little vine infested cemetery with tombstones too old to read without feeling the letters. It was next to an African Methodist Episcopal Church that looked slightly younger than the cemetery – Raphael Broad Max AME Church. About a mile or so west of the hotel and across the river near Mission Woods was a bar-b-que restaurant called Kevin's Place. All the clues seemed to fit, but then not at all.

They had courtesy computers and Internet access in the office lounge of the hotel. He searched the 2016 Web for clues about Savannah. What he found was an entire string of conspiracy theories around rooms 138 in hotels across America. Some thought it was a devil worshipping cult. Others thought it was a secret society or government cover-up. Stories of strange men and women always breaking into or seeking out room 138 filled these webpages on the subject. There were grisly stories of human sacrifices. Some of the stories claimed these 138 invaders were ghosts or demons. He found not one person who speculated it might be time travelers.

So much for not leaving a footprint. We've become Bigfoot instead.

Hank finally tried to go to bed.

At 1:00 AM on August 16th, a break-in went bad not far from Kevin's Place and a couple kids got shot. Hank would end up looking it up later in September a couple years in the future. He never found out what happened to the gunmen. The kids died, but the gunmen didn't know it, yet. The robbers and killers scattered. Hank woke at 2:00 AM, realizing he hadn't ported again that night, and anxiety turned to insomnia. New York and Kansas City bounced back and forth inside his skull. Would he be stuck in 2016 forever, and would that be worse than continuing to port? What else might happen if he got disconnected from the ports and his movement through time? He didn't know, but at the same time he just knew it was bad. He knew it on a lizard brain level where the fear of snakes and spiders was kept.

He took a walk at 4:30 AM. His walk ended at 4:46, and he stood at the door of room 138 of the Raphael fumbling with his keycard with a gun to the back of his head at 4:54.

"Christ sake, you better open …" The janky white kid cut off as the lock went green, and the door swung in. He pushed Hank inside and slammed the door behind them. "Don't turn around. Don't think about turning around."

The kid breathed hard stalking in a tight circle, like a caged animal. Hank couldn't see him, but heard him hitting his head with something. Maybe the gun. Not a word, but the voice went high and squeaky with the air coming in and out of his throat. He had to be 6'7" and thin as a rail, so the tight space between the bathroom and door of the suite only gave him about a step and a half on each lap of his circuit.

"I didn't … It was … I didn't have nothing to do with … I didn't … I didn't …"

"You didn't what?"

The silence that followed felt cold. Hank almost shivered before the butt of the gun struck the back of his skull and knocked him forward a couple steps. He waited to black out or fall down, but he didn't. The hot flow of blood he expected through his hair and down his neck didn't come either. It took a second, but the throbbing pain in the back of his head finally filled in. At that point, he waited on a bullet and darkness.

Maybe this is what happens when you miss a port.

"I wasn't talking to you. Shut up your talking. Sit down. Sit down on the bed before I … just sit down there on the corner and face that way. Don't look at me. Don't look at me. Don't say anything. Don't say another word. Don't do anything … Do you think anyone saw us? … I asked you a question. Do you think anyone saw us coming up?"

Hank took a deep breath. "No, it's four in the morning. No one saw."

"It's five."

"Okay, but no one saw us. You're good."

"I saw people checking out when we came in that side door. There were people."

"They were handling their own bags and kids. No one saw you."

"I'm not exactly dressed for a place like this, and I got blood on my shirt and shorts."

Hank swallowed and said, "No one saw. If we stay quiet, no one will even know you're in here."

"Right. Okay. I didn't shoot anyone. Not this time. Kevin shot them or maybe Raphael, but I didn't shoot anyone. I was just standing there."

The names bothered Hank. Partly because it felt surreal to hear them repeated in a situation like this. The universe seemed … contrived. Badly designed. A sick riddle coming undone. Partly, he was bothered because the guy might be planning to kill him, if he was throwing around his buddies' names, or if he suddenly realized he had done it. "You're good then. We're good."

Silence. Then, more squeaking, shuffling, and clacking the gun against his head. *I'll bounce that gun off your skull for you, kid. Least I could do.*

"No. No, it's not good. No. They'll bust me just for being there. That's how it works. We all go down. They catch one of us. They catch all of us. We're all busted for it. I could … hop a train … No, I'm … No …"

"Then, we make sure you don't get caught. You stay in here until everything cools down, and then we get you out of town."

"What?"

"You hide here, and no one finds us. We're good."

"There's no 'we.' We're not boys, Boy. We're not in this together, so don't start that mind … Don't start. Don't try me, Son."

"Okay."

"I'm still a little buzzed, and I'm paranoid as hell, so don't start with me. Don't!"

"Okay."

More pacing.

The sun broke the horizon to the left of the window,

and Hank nodded on the edge of the bed. *Can't sleep on a soft bed in the quiet, but I can go to sleep sitting up with a murderer fidgeting behind me. Just great.*

"Go look out the window. What's out there? Tell me."

Hank startled full awake and stood up. His legs tingled and shook under him. He had to focus to make his feet move.

"Don't try anything. Don't."

"I'm not. I won't." He stared out at the river and traffic. There were a few joggers. A peloton of cyclists with helmets and skintight clothes pedaled along in a line, holding up the cars behind them. "Nothing. There's nothing going on. Just normal morning stuff."

"Don't lie. Don't."

"I'm not."

"I can hear a siren. I hear it."

Hank didn't hear anything. "Must be far away. There's nothing out here. They're not coming here. They don't know you're here."

"It could be out front on the other side."

"This is the front of the hotel."

"Then out the back!"

"There's no one here. No one saw you."

"I'm sorry. I don't have any other choice here. Just keep staring out the window, okay? It won't hurt. You won't even know it happened."

Jesus ...

Hank turned around and held up his hands. The

dude was shaking like one of those little dogs rich people bred the wolf out of and just sat on pillows all day. His eyes went wide, and he raised the gun at Hank's face. Now the dude looked more like a wolf again. Or maybe a starved, rabid coyote.

"Told you not to look at me. Turn back around."

"If you fire the gun, people will hear and call the cops. You're safe now. Don't screw that up."

"Turn around or I'll shoot you in the face instead of the back of the head."

"You screw up your hiding spot, if you shoot. Just don't shoot, and no one will ever know you're here. You can rest. We can call room service. You're safe as long as we both stay quiet."

The guy's eyes darted back and forth. The pupils shook when he tried to look to the side. He advanced on Hank from around the bed in four long strides with his skinny, quivering gun arm extended out. Hank's shoulders hit the glass as he recoiled and winced. "No, don't. Don't. Don't …"

The guy stopped with the bore of the gun a foot from Hank's face. He thought this might be his only chance to grab it, but pressed his elbows into his own ribs on both sides and his muscles locked on him. He felt the ache of old bruises on his sides. "Don't, man. You don't have to."

"I do." The guy backed away and grabbed a pillow from the bed. He tossed it across, and it landed heavy at Hank's feet. "Pick it up and put it over your face."

"No."

The guy took a couple short steps closer. "Put it over your face, so I can do this quiet. Do it. I'm running out of patience. Just do what I say so this can be over. I just want it over. Please, put the pillow over your face."

Hank picked it up, and the guy took another step forward.

Hank launched it with both hands, and the pillow seemed to be as heavy as stone. It moved in slow motion through the air before the gun roared and the bullet thumped through the pillow. He expected the air to fill with feathers, but that didn't happen. Glass shattered behind him.

Hank charged, but felt like he was moving in slow motion, too. The gun went off again. He tensed, but felt nothing as he collided with the rail-thin gunman. They danced back and forward with limbs twisting and knees striking. The gun roared a third time into the ceiling. Someone screamed outside the room, but not from above.

Hank staggered backward, smelling the guy's rancid breath hot over his face. His elbow cleared more glass from the broken window. The guy tried to headbutt and struck the corner of the window frame instead of Hank. He barked out a stinking curse and covered his face with his hand. Hank headbutted the back of the guy's hand over his nose and heard another barked curse.

Twisting the gun hand, Hank ran the guy's forearm along the broken glass, still clinging in the window, drawing blood. The gun went off again out over the river and tumbled out of his grasp. Hank felt relief until he started getting punched in the side of the head. Hank punched back, missing more than he hit.

Greasy thumbs clawed at Hank's eyes. Hank took hold of the guy's head and pushed him down into the glass, slicing open an eyelid. The guy screamed and pulled away.

His elbow cracked the flatscreen on the dresser. The TV wobbled, but didn't fall. The guy rolled two times on the floor and charged face first into the door. It sounded as loud as the gunshots. He clawed the door open and disappeared.

Hank felt dizzy as he watched the door drift closed in slow motion. Lights flickered in the corners of his vision, and he felt the room coming unglued from time. "Now?"

He wavered on his feet, leaving the broken window behind. Finally, he closed his hand over the strap of his satchel next to the broken TV.

Hank looked down and saw blood draining slick along his left sleeve and across his chest over his shirt. "Oh, God …"

Was he porting, or was this what dying felt like? It would make sense that death would work like a port. His vision darkened. He hit his knee against the brilliant white footboard of the bed and collapsed onto the plush comforter at an angle, staining the white fabric beyond saving.

He clutched the satchel to his chest with the fingers of his left hand going numb, as he stared at the bullet hole in the ceiling.

Someone knocked on the door. No, they pounded on the door and yelled. Or maybe he was still getting punched. Sirens were closer now. The janky white dude was right about the sirens. The room spun, and nausea spun the other direction in his stomach.

The ceiling faded into a spiral, a kaleidoscope of colors. A rocket train flew out from the center toward the edges.

Let's try again. What do you see?

Hank pursed his lips and made a wet static sound with his mouth for the flying train's rocket.

His shoulder burned and stung, but then he felt and saw nothing at all.

Chapter 10

August 17, 1916 - Saturela, New Mexico

Hank watched the family move in a panic. The wife took the two kids' arms above their elbows like she was trying to twist them off.

The father stuffed suitcases under his arms. "Go. Go. Just go!"

The kids screamed and cried as the mother dragged them bodily out the open door into a washout of white-hot sunlight. Hank couldn't feel the heat from it yet as he stood invisible and unfinished in the corner. The room was plain and the drapes over the window next to him hung threadbare and transparent. The mother screamed and cried, along with her kids, loud enough to hear from outside.

The father looked about the room with his arms hooked around the luggage and his back hunched.

His eyes were wide and darty in a way that reminded Hank of the janky white guy – the guy who just shot him. Hank tried to shiver, but couldn't do it yet. He didn't feel anything in his shoulder either, so maybe the wound didn't port with him. If the satchel came with everything in it, then a bullet embedded in his shoulder would, too. Just the blood he spilled would be left behind in 2016.

The father ran, but was too wide for the door. One big leather suitcase collided with the wall and shot out of his grasp behind him. The case blasted open as the metal latches gave out upon impact, and dumped the contents out across the thin carpet. It was mostly clothes, but he saw some dollar bills spread out on the floor.

Hank felt sure the man would come back for this, but the seconds ticked by. He would know for sure once he became solid again. The searing pain through his shoulder announced his welcome to 1916. Hank dropped to one knee and groaned as the pain and hotbox heat of the room struck him at once.

Glass shattered out of the window above him, and Hank braced himself to be punched again. Plaster blasted away in dramatic fashion beside him, and a bullet punched dull into the mattress. Gunshots cracked off outside, and more bullets hit, but he couldn't see where.

Am I getting shot at in every century now?

Hank went to duck down and crawl, but searing pain raced out from his shoulder. He fell to both knees, weak against the wall. Shots continued to fire, but none broke through the walls this time.

He got to his feet and hobbled to the suitcase. With one arm, he grabbed up the money, some clothes, and a pile of letters still in their envelopes. He didn't bother to read anything, but just stuffed it all into his satchel. He might need the clues, if he survived.

Shielding his eyes from the blinding sun, he stepped out into the sharper heat of the outside. Something exploded some distance to the right. Wind scoured the front of the cottage and shrapnel rained down on the roof. He thought about ducking back inside, but more bullets peppered the cottage.

What is this? What's going on?

Hank ran through the street and between two single story buildings across the way. He growled against the pain of his wound, and his neck started to cramp on that side.

"Stop!" Two uniformed soldiers aimed at him from the next dirt street. They wore khaki material and cloth hats. Their guns were bolt action rifles.

The second soldier said, "You with Villa's men?"

Hank had no idea what to say. He held up one hand, but the other wouldn't respond. "Um, no … No."

The second soldier said, "They say 'no' in Spanish, too, you know."

The first soldier pronounced the "H's" as he asked, "Habla English, Hombre?"

"I'm American," Hank said. "My name's Hank. I

was in my room when the shooting started. I got hit. I was just passing through on my way to …" *Is California a state yet? Sure, it is. I think.* "… California. Going to see my aunt and uncle. What's happening?"

"Come with us. Keep your head down."

"Medic," the other shouted. "Medic. Another Civvy."

They guided him through the streets. Two more explosions went off behind them.

"What war is this? On American soil?" Hank said.

"It is a flap," one of the soldiers said. "Spigotty bandits are going to pay high with their greasy lives. By Jack, this will not be another Columbus."

Hank didn't know what they meant, but he was left with uniformed medical corps and plain clothes people tending the wounded. They sat him down on a low section of stone wall. A woman tore open Hank's shirt at the shoulder. Blood had soaked through that side.

She splashed water over his wound twice, and Hank cried out.

"Sorry. I have to be able to see."

Hank looked down into the dirty bucket she had used for the water and cringed.

"It went all the way through. Almost a graze. No bone hit. Really small holes, too. You are lucky."

Hank said, "I …" Then, he screamed.

She pressed bandages on both sides and wrapped his shoulder tight. "Come now. You're a stronger man than that. Hold tight, Sam."

Hank braced himself. He hoped he was porting soon to somewhere that could treat infection before he died of some blood poisoning or got lockjaw. He had found over a few illnesses and several ports that healthcare that mattered was late twentieth century at best. And Savannah had insisted they needed to get to the early 2000's or later for the antibiotics to do any good. Anything earlier wasn't strong enough, she said. Maybe that was a clue as to when he was originally from, or maybe it just meant he had jumped around and was exposed to too many germs for 1990's antibiotics to do the trick anymore.

"Your face is bruised and swelling. You're well spotted and scratched around your ribs on this side as well. Did you fall or get hit by something?" She used one finger to lift his shirt where she had torn it down the side when she ripped away his sleeve.

"I ... I don't remember. Maybe." He could almost smell the janky white guy's rotten breath again.

She finished his shoulder and stepped away to tend to other wounded. People with burns rode into the medical area on stretchers. The wrap was tight, and his shoulder throbbed hot underneath. His hand was numb, but he could still move the fingers.

The gunfire continued, but at a greater distance than before.

A child with a wooden bucket on his hip stopped in front of Hank. His throat was dry, and the sun cooked him, so he tried not to think about parasites, as the boy ladled water over Hank's lips. Some spilled down the front of his torn shirt, but Hank didn't care as he swallowed slowly.

"Should have gone to New York like you was s'posed to."

Hank froze with a bit of water still in his mouth. He turned and saw the water carrier wasn't a kid. The dark-haired dwarf moved between the other wounded and out of the medical area without offering anyone else a drink.

Hank coughed and choked on the last of the water. He gritted his teeth as he stood.

A hand on his good shoulder guided him back down to seated. She said, "You just sit a spell and be still. There is nowhere you need to go for now."

Hank lost track of the dwarf between buildings. He bowed his head and used his satchel to shade himself. His head still throbbed from getting hit by the gun and fists a hundred years in the future.

Chapter 11

October 31, 1984 - Leonardo, New Jersey

The last chance of it being a warm Fall had disappeared with the last of the leaves, all disbursed on the ground with the cold wind.

Hank walked the streets, not knowing where he was going. The small hotel room he'd ended up in offered no clues to his next port or how long he'd be here.

The fact it was Halloween was an interesting one. For the last few weeks he'd been trapped in 1916, slowly moving east because the clues had pointed him in that direction.

Was it the right direction? Now he wasn't so sure. He'd seen the dwarf once but then not again, even though the small man was in the same place and time. Why? What was the point of announcing his presence?

In this year, the children were out early for Halloween, mostly in costumes their mothers had made. They carried pillowcases instead of expensive store-bought specialty plastic pumpkins with company logos on the sides. Groups of children roamed the streets, excited for a large haul of candy.

One woman was dressed as a nun. She had children in various costumes with her. Hank watched them as they went by. Something stuck in his mind. It was something intense, but there was no detail to it. If it was a feeling attached to a memory, he wasn't pulling it up.

He stood there for a long moment before his thoughts moved on from the feeling that this was important.

Hank wondered if Trick or Treat had been a big deal when he was a kid. He thought it had to have been, since even now he wanted to knock on a stranger's door, yell *trick or treat* and get a Snickers bar. Maybe a full-sized candy bar in this time frame. When did they start up with that "fun sized" nonsense? They probably still gave out homemade baked goods in this time with no fear of strangers trying to hurt their kids with razorblades or pot brownies.

He kept walking, lost in his thoughts. Where had Savannah ended up? Had the dwarf bothered her as well?

Now Hank was wondering if he'd made the wrong port. It wasn't something he'd considered in the past. He always thought it was port or no port. But was that how this all worked? Maybe he'd end up trapped in

1984 and never figure out about the dwarf, Savannah, and why he'd been porting in the first place.

Hank stopped walking and shook his head, probably looking odd to the children flowing past. "Why am I so sure not being at the right room 138 to port will keep me trapped in a place?"

He'd lost any identity he once had, his past, and his real name. Yet one of the things he knew from the beginning, this new beginning, was which innocuous things were clues and which ones mattered to get him to the next jump-off.

Hank kept walking for what felt like hours until he came to a main area of town and spied the perfect place to get out of the cold and do some more thinking.

The Junction Liquors had a bar area.

"All aboard," Hank whispered as he went inside.

It was currently unoccupied by drinkers, but the bartender, a slim woman with a scar running from under her right eye to her ample bosom, was looking busy washing and rewashing the same four glasses.

Hank sat and put his satchel on the stool next to him.

"If we suddenly get crowded, put that underneath your seat," she said with a wink and laugh. "What'll ya have?"

"What's the finest and cheapest beer on tap in Leonardo?"

She shook her head. "You're in Belford now. The Navy bridge you passed is what separates Belford from Leonardo. Weapons Station Earle. Except for that landmark you really can't tell a difference. Where ya from?"

All aboard, Weapons Station Earle, he thought.

Hank had no idea. "I travel a lot."

She was using one of the just-cleaned glasses to fill with Budweiser. "Salesman?"

"Propane and propane accessories," he said in his Hank Hill voice, which got a weird look from her. He guessed *King of The Hill* was still a few years from being on TV. "I stayed in Leonardo last night."

She chuckled. "There's only one place to stay, so I know where. Once you get further north into Hazlet and Keyport, you'll find a few more options." She put the beer in front of Hank and raised a finger.

Hank pulled out a five dollar bill, quickly scanning it to make sure it was dated 1984 or earlier. He'd reset his wallet with the proper cash, but it was one of his habits to double-check. Especially with his mind still reeling from his encounter with the dwarf and recovering from a gunshot wound, he couldn't be too careful.

She rang the register and put four singles on the bar next to his glass and went back to cleaning the clean glasses.

Hank needed to figure out his next move. He'd arrived via port this morning, but nothing out of the ordinary had happened. The previous residents of the motel room had already left, but he found five twenties stuffed in a sock they'd forgotten.

There were also two Stephen King novels and a Brian C. Redd novel. The Redd novel was one of his weird sci fi books. He had apparently entered that phase of his writing career by this year. *Green Water Elves of the Great Spiral* was not one of his best works. So far, nothing about the dog-eared paperbacks had jumped out at him, although he figured he might read them to pass the time.

"Aren't you going to ask me? Everyone does," the bartender said and pointed at her scarred face.

Hank shrugged. "I wasn't going to be rude."

"Rude is not asking about it." She smiled. "It's a conversation starter, especially when people are drunk. I got it as a child. Fell off my bike."

Hank nodded slowly. He really wasn't interested in small talk. He'd come into the bar thinking he'd get a couple of beers in him and be able to figure a few things out, not have to talk to the bartender.

She laughed. "You believe that? Falling off a bike can do this much damage to someone?"

"I have no idea." Hank also had no idea if he knew how to ride a bike. He was sure he did. All kids were taught to ride a bike. Right? "Maybe you fell on some glass."

"Maybe my father sliced me up in a drunken rage," she said with a smile, as if it was nothing. She was still cleaning the same glasses, which Hank was starting to see as very odd behavior. "Perhaps I was in a knife fight in prison. Was pushed into a barbed wire fence.

Attacked by a mad butcher with a chainsaw." She was still smiling.

"I'm guessing only you and whoever did that really knows what happened," Hank said for something to say because she was staring at him.

She finally put the glass and dishrag down and stood in front of him. She put her thumbs on either side of her shirt near the top of her chest and pulled it forward, offering Hank a generous showing of her cleavage. "See how far it goes down?"

Hank turned away, but he'd seen more than enough. It went down towards her stomach and maybe further south.

"I got this scar in 1916," she whispered. "In New Mexico."

Hank turned back, his mouth agape. "What did you say?"

She walked away, but kept eye contact. "You heard me." At the end of the bar she pointed. "You have a visitor. Make this quick. I need to get back to my real work."

Hank, still shocked, turned to see someone who he'd describe as a mobster, wearing a fedora over his slicked back hair. He had a toothpick in his mouth and a dark gray coat on over his navy blue suit. He was seated at the corner table, back to the wall and staring at Hank.

"Bring over the bottle of bourbon," the man said to Hank. He held up two fingers. "And glasses."

The bartender had disappeared. Hank went around the bar and got the items, expecting someone to stop him. No one did. He sat across from the man.

"You pour. I'll talk. We don't have a lot of time." The man spoke to Hank, but watched the door. "If I get up and leave, do yourself a favor and don't let whoever came through the door capture you."

"Who are you?"

The man put up a hand. "I talk. You pour. Generously."

Hank poured, making sure the man had more in his glass. The last thing Hank wanted was to get drunk. He opened his mouth to ask the first of a hundred questions, but stopped himself.

"I'm a friend, whether you'll believe it or not after we speak. I know you from before all of this." The man put up his hand. "No questions. Next visit, whenever that will be. They're not far behind me. If they catch us together, we're both dead. Just… listen. Please."

Hank nodded and took a small sip of his drink.

The man didn't touch his glass. "You can call me Terry. Not my real name. I'm not going to take a chance that using my real name will elicit a subconscious response inside you, and you might remember who you really are, which is a very bad thing at this point in your journey."

"Why?"

"It's not time. You were clear about that. The only way you can actually complete porting is if you finish what we started this time. You'll remember then." Terry smiled and ran a finger around the rim of his glass. "You've been built in with many false memories and purposeful holes in the puzzle. Sometimes those have to be reinforced. Things that have never really happened are mixed in with the real stuff. So much so, it's hard to decipher real from fantasy. To control what you do, false notions have been added, wired in. You need to keep moving and porting, or you'll be stuck. Bad things will happen for all of us. All of us. You get me?" He shook his head. "But the clues aren't always what they seem, and there's not just one track forward. The universe is more complex than all that."

Hank shook his head. This was too much. "But…"

Terry sighed. "There are dozens of us. Some assigned to other parts of the world. The bulk in Europe and Africa. A lot of land to cover. We keep traveling the loop for them."

"To do what?"

"Searching for someone or something. I'm not sure. No one has been able to figure it all out, yet. You aren't missing blocks of time; you lose chunks out of the middle and then the pieces shuffle. We get too close, then we have to start over. It's been a long loop this time. Only the designer understands it. Somewhere, buried deep in our programming, we'll know when we see it. Maybe. Then, it starts again." Terry shook his head and downed his drink in one gulp, wincing as he put the glass back on the table and motioned for Hank to fill it again. "Do you trust Savannah?"

He felt a chill run through him at the mention of her name.

"Yes," Hank said immediately.

"Have you met the dwarf?"

"Yes. Recently. For a brief moment."

"What about Mister Train?"

Hank shook his head. "I don't know who that is."

Terry shrugged. "You might never meet him. That wouldn't be a bad thing." He glanced at the door again. "I'm going to give you this." Terry pulled out a sheet of paper from his pocket. "It has the clues for your next port, if that's what you're calling it."

He put it on the table, and Hank looked at it.

"It has two sets of clues… one leading to Menomonie in Wisconsin and the other to Lebanon in Kansas. Don't ask me where they came from. It's a course adjustment that came from someone who knows better. It's to get you back on track. There are forces working against us and would see us all dead before this is finished."

"Who?" Hank asked. "Who are you worried about?"

Terry shook his head. "I'd suggest writing down any questions you have for me for our next meeting, if it ever happens. We might never be in the same slipstream together. Always a different port of call or jumping off point or slipstream exit. Whatever you want to call it, there are only so many options available in each time, even though we all follow the same date structure."

"You've lost me," admitted Hank.

Terry tapped on the piece of paper. "If you trust Savannah and believe the dwarf is going to harm you, I'd head to Menomonie. If you're thinking Savannah is part of the problem and not the solution, and the dwarf didn't harm you because he's on your side, you should go to Lebanon. You have three days to get to whichever one you need to get to. In either place you'll find something interesting your brain will try to discredit or dismiss. I need you to stay focused. This is critical. If you arrive on November fourth, don't get a room 138 until the sixth. It will give you time to get a better understanding of what you need to do going forward." Terry finished the second glass and smacked his lips. He stood and grabbed the bottle. "If you choose the right path, of course."

Hank wanted to scream. "Tell me the right track."

Terry shook his head. "I can't. If I did that, it would change everything. Only you can choose the right way. Remember that. If someone tries to push you in a certain direction or track, it's because they've either been sent to do it, or they're one of us and trying to get you to stay in the loop and do whatever we're supposed to be doing."

"What happens when I deviate from the path? What if I refuse to choose either place?"

Terry was already headed to the door. "It doesn't work that way. They're here. Sneak out the back. I'll get you some time."

"I don't understand."

"You will." Terry smiled. "I'm glad I got to see you again."

Hank heard several vehicles pulling up in the parking lot and fled to the rear of the building, through the stockroom and out the back door. He climbed a fence into a backlot of a gas station and over the far fence into a residential yard, past a swing set and sandbox and onto a side street.

He swung back around and came up behind Martin's Garage, between a 7-Eleven and an ice cream place. Hank decided to go inside for an ice cream, so he could watch out the window.

By the time he was done selecting a chocolate ice cream in a cone and sat down at a table near the window, he heard the sirens.

Four matching black SUV's sped by in a line, windows tinted so he couldn't even see the driver.

Two Middletown Police vehicles and an ambulance went by, pulling into where he guessed the Junction Liquors was. At this angle he couldn't see anything.

Hank walked over to the gas station, acting casual and eating his melting ice cream. He didn't want to get too close.

He didn't need to.

The spilled alcohol was what he smelled first, but the blood soon overpowered it.

"Robbery attempt. He shot the bartender inside," one of the cops was saying. "She shot him in the back as she fell."

Hank knew he'd never have a chance to ask follow-up questions with Terry. He felt sad for the bartender, who'd had a tough life, whatever it had been.

Now he needed to get as far away from New Jersey as possible and figure out which path was the right one.

Chapter 12

November 3, 2008 - New York

Hank slid the box over and went into another. He took out a composition notebook with a faded pink marbled cover. Some patches on the back were still a brighter red. It was spotted with white mold and the black taped spine peeled away in shredded threads. The pages were stiff, brittle, and yellowed. He recognized his own handwriting, but not the words or the notebook itself.

In the back of the storage unit, a few ruined guns sat. They hadn't been protected from the elements. A generator sat back there in bad condition, too. Three gold bars had been stacked between the guns. *Imagine walking into a bank or a pawn shop trying to exchange those without answering any questions?*

He had stopped taking notes countless ports ago, but here were more notebooks than he remembered, written margin to margin with nearly no paragraph breaks. The sentences didn't lead one into another. Sometimes there were random facts – some historical and some personal. Many sentences were incomplete and used abbreviations or shorthand he couldn't decipher.

This ancient pink-red notebook ran from January 12 – August 23 according to the cover, but the years inside it jumped around from dates over a century apart in some cases. Some were much too early for a notebook like this to be used as a diary. He had no way of knowing how many years back this edition was along his timeline. He didn't recall it at all. None of the locations or details rang a bell. On his journey, the dates stayed in order, but the years followed their own rules. Unless he thought to start counting his personal years, he'd never know. He might not have the memory to achieve that. That might be on purpose by some shady organization's design, if he could believe anything he had been told.

He looked up from an alien entry in his own handwriting and scanned over the moldering boxes. There were over a dozen more than he remembered from the last time he had been here, just a few years in the future – more than he ever recalled any other time he made it to New York.

Maybe he needed to get a more weatherproof storage unit, but he'd already been to this one multiple times in the past and in the future. He was stuck with this place.

Nothing made sense anymore. Terry? Savannah? The dwarf? Mr. Choo Choo? A young dead bartender with a 70-year-old scar who died 24 years ago and just three days ago on Halloween? That had been a Wednesday. Three days later it was now a Monday in a different millennium.

As he stared at the shadows in the old brick walls of his storage unit, the radio sitting behind him came back from a commercial break. Through the radio's speaker belted the echoing voice of a woman who was running for Vice President in tomorrow's election. He couldn't remember her name, even though it had been said a few times while he had been sitting here. He couldn't remember a lot of things. There had been a woman running for Vice President during Halloween in 1984, hadn't there? Maybe there was a connection and a clue there. In a couple decades, another woman became Vice President in front of a field of flags like grave markers, where hardly anyone sat, as everyone wore masks during one of the deadliest stretches of years to port into. He should look up their names, he thought. He couldn't recall much useful peripheral detail since he had been given cryptic instructions by a strange time traveler – stranger than Hank himself. And then, of course, there was the murder of the bartender time traveler, too.

Why would time travel hunters need SUVs? What did they drive when they were in the early 20th century?

The 2008 Vice Presidential hopeful echoed out of the radio's single speaker from some rally in a swing state. She was talking about something her opponent had said in San Francisco about clinging to guns.

Was it San Francisco this time? Was that where he was supposed to go?

Before this, he had to choose from Nowhere, Kansas or Nowhere, Wisconsin because "Terry" had told him so. He did choose one, and nothing went right. Every sign pointed the other way. Every single one. Either they were trying to confuse him or trying to help him, but how could he know? He kept going even though he knew deep down his choice had to be wrong. If he showed up after the fourth, he was supposed to wait until the sixth, but he showed up on the damn second, so now what?

He flipped to a random page. *Rusty Nail or Salt Lake?* The question was circled three times and the pen marks split the paper in a couple spots. Underneath the circled question, still in his handwriting, but in faded pencil and calmer: *You've tried this twice. You have to find another way in or it just starts over. Another cycle of lies.* There was more, but it was too smudged and faded to read.

Closing that notebook, he rubbed his fingers over the cover.

He came to his storage unit in New York, looking for answers. He angrily flipped through the brittle pages without being careful of their age. He had given up trying to read them all. He just scanned for Terry …

for Savannah … for Mr. Train … for references to the dwarf. He occasionally saw other names and paused. The text on either side didn't help much for context. Sometimes he recognized famous names from history, but had no idea why he had written them. Other names just hung there in the endless paragraphs without any explanation, so he flipped on through the pages. So much of it was ramblings about possible clues which meant so much at the time, but were pointless to him decades later or decades earlier in a few cases.

Someone was interviewing a Governor Romney on the radio. Hank listened for a moment. The name sounded familiar. Something from Michigan in the 60's? How many ports ago? He couldn't begin to count. This wasn't the guy running for President this time, though. They were asking him if the McCain campaign had been "run with decency," whatever that meant. Romney pivoted to say the Obama campaign was the nasty one.

Hank stopped listening again.

He tossed aside the marbled pink and picked up a journal with a moleskin cover. The material was matted flat and rubbed into smooth black patches in several places. The yellowed pages had a few more paragraphs, but made just as little sense as the previous journal and the previous boxes of journals before that. This one did not have the dates labeled clearly. It was still his handwriting, so he scanned through his madman ravings in this copy, too.

Romney concluded before the next commercial

break by saying that he hoped Obama's campaign and his supporters in Chicago had a long cold night.

Was Chicago the next port? Hank shook his head. He wished the music stations came in clearer, but he didn't want to sit outside the unit. Elections bugged him. It was too much noise to think clearly and find the clues. He had ported into a few election seasons. Everyone was so intense and intent that this was the difference between life and death, every time, in every decade. In many cases, he already recalled who won and what happened afterward. It was literally history for him.

He couldn't recall who won the 2008 election. Neither name jumped out at him this time. There were a bunch of elections before and after the turn of the century that blended together for him. Nothing much important happened really until the 2020s. That decade started bad and ended worse. Then, a war?

He recalled an election earlier in the 20th century he had been present for. He didn't recall who won then, either. There had been bands, and pie, and dancing, and fireworks. Everyone seemed to be having such a great time and …

Something squeaked outside. Hank dropped the journal and walked to the door. A young man with dirty hair was pushing a cart away from Hank's unit, down the line to the left. There were empty plastic jugs and hoses on it. Meth? A bomb?

Hank ducked back inside. He wanted zero trouble. Getting involved in anything suspicious in New York after 2001 was bad news. You could walk down the street and practically commit a crime in broad daylight in the 70s, but you carry a satchel with strange combinations of dollars inside in early 2002, and you might never go free.

He finished the box and moved to the next. This one was filled with old paperback novels. There were a lot of Brian C. Redd books. *Port of Call* was in here, a dog-eared copy of *The Couple from Nowhere*, the *Salt Lake Wasteland* one, a crazy ass horror book Redd wrote in the mid-seventies called *Nazi Time Traveling Acid Rock Dwarves*, *Rusty Headed Dreams* from the late 90s, *The Mojave Salt Flats* was a good and classic Brian Redd crime novel, and *Scorpion Kisses Beside the Virgin River* was a great crime fiction read.

Hank squinted as he picked up *Scorpion Kisses*. He flipped to the copyright page. This book wasn't published until 2011. He started to put it in his satchel, but stopped. Was it worse to leave a book from the future in here or to carry it all through time?

The book opened to a page marked by a white plastic card. Hank lifted the marker out and examined it. He remembered this. He had no idea what it was for, but he recalled it being in his satchel from as far back as he could remember. At one point, it had been his biggest obsession about his identity. It had to mean something, this plain plastic card. At some point, while reading *Scorpion Kisses* by Brian C. Redd in 2011, he'd marked his place in the book with the mysterious card, forgotten about it, and dropped the book off here for storage.

Turns out the little card he obsessed over for all that time hadn't been something he had found a use for since. After a moment, Hank kept the card, tossed the future book back into the box, and pushed the box of Redd novels aside.

In the next box of notebooks, the first journal he opened was only half finished and started on November 15 Two-thousand and something. The pencil markings were badly faded and smeared on the first page. He could tell from holding it that a number of pages had been torn out of the middle in multiple places. It was the message in blue pen on the inside of the cover that caught his attention: *If you haven't lived this yet, don't read it. But start writing the journals again.*

It looked like his handwriting. He tossed the journal down and picked up another with a number of pages missing and a damaged cover. This time in black ink on the inside cover: *Stop writing the journals. And stop coming here. Go find her so this can …*

The bottom of the cover and the rest of the message were missing. Hank threw it down and held his head. "What the hell?"

With the cover missing, he read the bottom lines of the first page: *The Clocksmiths are much more trouble this time around. Maybe our loops are making them worse. The cellphone from Penn. isn't …*

Hank didn't bother to turn the page to keep reading. It wouldn't make sense to him anyway.

He stepped outside of the storage unit just in time

for the dirty guy to push his squeaky cart back toward him. The jugs were full of water now. Or a clear liquid at least. The guy opened a unit a few doors down from Hank's. The guy looked familiar, but Hank couldn't place him.

The door opened, and Hank saw a bunk, a stove, and a TV inside the unit that was on but muted. The dude was living in there. That had to be cheaper than the way Hank was living.

"What're you staring at, stranger?"

The voice sounded familiar. Terry? He looked different, but it was him. Hank took a step toward him and reached in his pocket.

The guy brought up his fists scarred with scratches. "Don't do it, stranger."

Hank stopped. "I wrote down my questions for the next time we met, like you said."

"You did?"

"Yeah, Terry, I have a few more, too. Wenomonie, Wisconsin or Lebanon, Kansas. One if I trusted Savannah. The other if I thought the dwarf was after me like she thinks or something like that. I chose Wisconsin because I wanted to believe in her. Everything along the way told me I was wrong, but I wanted to believe her, so I jumped the slipstream in Wisconsin. I still think it was the wrong port of call, but I chose to believe in her anyway. Now I don't know what to do, Terry. Tell me what to do."

"Dude?" The guy rolled his water cart into his

storage unit apartment. "You're crazy. I don't know you."

"Terry? You're supposed to guide me. What happened back at that bar after we left? Who were those people? Are they coming for us here, too?" Hank took another step and stopped. This kid was too young, over a decade too young. He sounded a little like Terry and looked like him a little, but that was it.

"I don't know you, man. I just woke up here a few days ago. I tried Utah, but I got too close. Messes it up for everybody, if you get too close. Stop messing with me. I don't know you."

"You're not Terry. Sorry." Hank said it as a flat statement.

"If I knew who I was, I wouldn't tell you." He slammed his door and left Hank standing there with his hand in his pocket, on a piece of paper, with unanswered questions.

Hank sighed and went back into his own unit. "I really did sound insane."

He searched the other boxes. If he had met Terry before, like the guy had claimed, he hadn't written about it.

The polls said Obama was going to win tomorrow, but it had already happened, or it hadn't, as far as Hank was concerned, so he didn't care either way. None of it mattered, just like his notebooks full of old clues didn't matter.

After he came up empty, he went back into the first

box where there had been a couple empty journals. He stuffed one into his satchel. He started writing in another about what had happened on Halloween. He started writing everything he could remember about Savannah, so he wouldn't forget, or so he could find it here again, if he did. He didn't bother using dates or paragraphs. It was getting late, so he started abbreviating wherever he could.

When he was in New York, he liked to eat in Central Park no matter what year or how cold it was. It was getting dark though, and he had long ago missed lunch, but he didn't want to be in the park that late. Maybe he'd go tomorrow, if the clues didn't point him out of town sooner.

Hank turned off the radio and removed the batteries from the back before boxing it.

He closed and locked up the unit as he stared down at Not Terry's door. So strange.

Hank said out loud, "I chose Wisconsin. Don't care if it was right. I want to believe her, and I'm going to find her. That's it. Whatever this is, we're getting out of it together or not at all."

He decided to try dinner at one of the bars. He knew all the TV's would be tuned to election coverage. It would be worse tomorrow, like watching a 48 hour rerun of the worst TV drama ever recorded. His head already ached just thinking about it.

Chapter 13

November 12, 2001 - Savannah, Georgia

Hank had an epiphany while standing in front of a restaurant, waiting for the tourists to clear a table so he could eat. The lines were ridiculous, although it was his own fault. He'd ported in and taken his time leaving the hotel, and when he finally got it together, he'd sat in the lobby for hours to think.

The previous hotel guests had left three thousand and change in an envelope under the mattress. He assumed they'd left it, or maybe it had been there for months or years without anyone noticing, even housekeeping.

Hank had stuck it in his pocket. He had several thousand dollars on him now, and all of it could be used in 2001. Money was never the issue as long as it was dated correctly. If bills were too old they might be valuable and would raise some eyebrows if he tried to use a 1915 twenty with Grover Cleveland on it instead of Jackson. They swapped them out in 1928.

Hank remembered a box in storage of pre-1928 twenties he might someday sell to collectors and make a killing. He thought he should probably do that before they decayed into a useless form like the guns, the generator, and most of the notebooks. He didn't recall seeing them as he dug through in 2008. He hoped those bills were still there. Maybe he was going to go get them here in 2001, and that's why they were gone a few days ago in 2008.

He blinked several times as his mind swirled around the complexity of time traveling.

Right now, he wanted a burger and a Coke. Did they have Diet Coke now? He thought so. Hank remembered getting sick a few times after a port when he'd eaten or drank a product he assumed was like every other one he'd ever had, only to learn they'd changed an ingredient or two that screwed with his stomach.

A table of smiling tourists finally paid their check and left. The waitress frowned when she saw it was only one person. Hank decided if she sucked it up and was nice, he'd give her a good tip to make up for it, even though he'd be a lot less work for her.

"Can you get me a pepper shaker, too, please?"

He ordered and began looking around, seeing if anything was going to be a clue for his next port.

Hank felt like all he did was search for the things

that jumped out for his next jump, and never really enjoyed where he was. Savannah, the city, had so much to offer, especially for someone with a few bucks in his pocket. The problem was always the timetable he was forced to adhere to so he didn't miss a port.

Even when he had weeks between ports, he never really knew. He felt the pressure when it was getting closer, and the clues were never easy to decipher at first. It would always be a last-minute decision to get to where he was headed for the next room 138, and he never got to stop and smell the flowers.

The wall of the restaurant was decorated with rusty railroad spikes.

"Appetizing stuff."

He'd driven through the night or ran through airports to catch a plane, or hopped on a train or Greyhound bus to get there on time, always in motion, even when he had time to kill.

Hank wanted to savor the moment, have a nice meal and a few hours of wandering a city and enjoying the sights. He could take in the tourist sight-seeing tours and have a cup of coffee in a park and people-watch until it was time to find a room for the night.

Just being normal for a few hours might make a world of difference.

He couldn't relax. Every time the door to the restaurant opened, he looked up, expecting to see someone he knew or someone he didn't want to have a cryptic conversation with.

If it was Savannah, the person, he didn't know how he'd act. Terry had cast doubt on her and the dwarf, and who was the friend and who the enemy. What if Hank was being manipulated? Of course, Terry could easily be the manipulator. He had talked like someone who knew and didn't know at the same time. Both couldn't be true. And who was trying to kill them? Were they just in 1980's New Jersey or everywhere in every time?

Hank almost wished for the early days he could remember, when he thought he was alone. He'd jump from year to year and spend all his time searching for clues, and it had been fun. Almost fun. Lonely, but simple. There wasn't danger and dwarves and false clues.

He'd felt like he was getting closer to solving a puzzle. As if he'd port and there would be the end of his journey. Balloons would fall from the ceiling. A crowd would cheer. He'd be showered in money and accolades for figuring it out, like he was at the Donkey Kong kill screen and there was nothing more to do.

Hank didn't remember ever playing video games, but he knew enough about Donkey Kong for some reason. It was another mystery. The notebooks filled with his rambling and writing was proof he'd done way more than he consciously knew.

He pictured a great countdown in over bright numbers lit up like the sun and tall enough to be the readout on God's watch. It was a countdown to the end of all of this. He wanted that ending. He wanted it deep in his bones.

Why? What was the point of all this?

Hank knew being in the city of Savannah and thinking about Savannah, the woman, might be a clue. It might be a coincidence, too. He always had a general feeling, but when he thought too hard about it, sometimes it would get jumbled.

Like the port he'd taken to Kansas City. When he thought now, it should've been to New York, based on the secondary clues. Was each port not a set destination, but a series of moves to have a choice? Choosing either Wisconsin or Kansas might have moved him onto a different track, but he was still moving along. The ports hadn't stopped. He could argue going to Menomonie instead of Lebanon had ported him into a corner, maybe a series of wrong turns he'd never recover from. What if Terry had purposely given him false clues to two ports he knew would screw Hank up?

Hank took a bite of his burger and tried to enjoy it. He needed to turn his brain off for a few hours. Enjoy his burger. Eat all his fries. Go window-shopping in a gorgeous city and get ice cream.

Relax. Enjoy the moment.

She never did bring him a pepper shaker.

Hank looked up when the door opened again and, for a split second, he thought Savannah had entered. It wasn't her. He let out his breath and shook his head.

After he'd eaten and left a good tip, he began wandering in random directions. He needed a distraction. Maybe a bookstore or a movie theater would do. He could find a pharmacy and a bottle of sleeping pills. He'd rent a room for the day and take a long, drug-addled nap and have his brain shut down for a while.

There was so much tie-dye in all the shop windows around here. Was it still the damn 1960s here? Each combination of color and white created more spirals.

Always in endless loops. My favorite.

Sleep without dreaming sounded good. No nightmares, no clues, no Savannah, and no dwarf would be a fine change of pace.

Hank glanced across the busy street and saw a woman wearing sunglasses and a hat pulled down, looking in his direction. She was standing in front of a model train shop called All Aboard, but she was looking at him, not in the shop window. She looked away when he stared back.

Who was she? It wasn't Savannah. Hank didn't recognize her, but he groaned. It was yet another player in this stupid game, someone else to confuse him. Cryptic words and no real clues were coming.

He had two choices: simply keep walking and ignore her, or rush across the street and confront the woman.

She turned away and began walking, lost in the crowd.

Hank wanted to scream.

Keep walking. She's gone. Out of sight. Out of mind, he thought, knowing he was lying to himself.

The traffic was now backed up, and he dashed

between the cars, careful not to get run down as he crossed the street.

Hank ran in the general direction she was headed, careful to not miss her, but keeping an eye on others who might also be following or watching.

Hank saw her ahead. She was walking hand in hand with a man he didn't recognize. Had the two of them been watching Hank, and now that she'd been spotted, they'd act like tourists and regroup for another pass at him later?

"Excuse me. Ma'am. Sir. Wait," Hank yelled. He was going to start turning over stones right here and right now, in public, in front of witnesses. "We need to talk."

They ignored Hank.

He ran in front of them and stopped. They nearly collided with him. The man looked annoyed, but registered no fear, no weird vibe coming from him.

Hank pointed at the woman. "Back there you were staring at me."

She frowned and lifted her sunglasses. "Excuse me?"

"What's this all about?" The man looked really annoyed now. His fists balled at his sides and Hank realized he was a big man. "Do we know you?"

"I think you do," Hank said, with growing doubt. They didn't look like they'd been caught. The guy was mad, but she looked genuinely curious. "You were staring at me."

"Where?" She looked back. "I was checking out the windows of the restaurants on the corner because I wanted to surprise my husband with a new place for dinner tonight." She smiled. "We've been in town three days, and he insists on eating at the hotel restaurant."

"I thought you liked it. You said you didn't care." The man's face softened and he took her hand.

Hank noticed the wedding rings. Either they were great actors or he was being paranoid.

Time travel psychosis … Post Porting Depression …

"I do like it but, jeez, we could not only explore Savannah walking around, but the rest of the cuisine, too." She hugged him. "That's all I'm saying."

"Uh, sorry for bothering you," Hank said.

She laughed. "No, thank you for saying something to me. It let me talk to my husband and tell him what was on my mind." She turned back to her man. "This is why we're here… to communicate and get away from life for a few days. To find ourselves again."

Hank smiled and walked away. The guy gave him a wave and went back to talking to his wife. They looked happy now. Free. Hank hoped they'd be able to work through their problems. He kept track of certain people in his notebooks that he found interested, with the hope to someday see them again and find out their progress.

Would this couple figure it all out? In five or ten years, were they long divorced and married to other people?

He walked, weaving in and out of tourists on the

crowded sidewalk. If he had the street to himself, he'd start to run. Get away, even though it was getting away from himself and his situation he really wanted.

It was all he could do not to scream in frustration. His paranoia had reached a new, daunting level.

Now he was confronting innocent people on the street, demanding they answer his crazy questions. He'd lucked out with the couple, especially since the guy had seemed so angry and capable of throwing a punch, but when would his luck end?

The next time he did something drastic, it could mean a beating or an arrest.

He couldn't live like this any longer.

Hank decided enough was enough. He'd make one last port, and then stay wherever it was, whenever it was.

He shook his head. That wouldn't work. If he ported to 1890, he'd be trapped there without modern conveniences and a lot of worthless money. He didn't think he was immortal. He felt like he was getting older, even though he had no true idea what age he was or for how long he'd been doing this.

Did he ever see changes in the mirror? Would he recognize aging, if he saw it?

What if he was unable to die? He'd once read a series of vampire books, and the main character hated being a vampire. He was bored. Living so many decades and trying to keep pace with the changes of the world was daunting.

Hank didn't want to live forever, especially if it meant having to port all the time and follow clues.

No more. It was over. He'd get to a time between the years 1975 and 2025 and be content. If future ports fell outside those years, he'd keep searching for the clues, keeping his head down and moving along, knowing it would eventually end.

He'd settle down. He had enough cash to live for a while. He figured he had some skills to use to get by. In New York City, he had boxes of not only notebooks but money and other precious items.

He could find himself a pretty wife and buy a nice house with a white picket fence. A couple of pets and a couple of kids could follow in time. He'd be the friendly neighbor who washed the car on Saturday and mowed the lawn on Sunday before a big dinner with the family.

Savannah and the dwarf and anyone else involved could go to Hell. They'd need to play this game without Hank. He wanted nothing more to do with them, and he was going to head out to find the clues to get him to the next and hopefully last port of his existence.

He wondered if any time traveler had tried this scheme of throwing in the towel before. Had they succeeded?

Chapter 14

November 14, 1969 - Portland, Maine

Hank kept looking up for a TV, but then had to remind himself it was a radio he was hearing in the background of the diner. Apollo 12 was set to launch in less than an hour according to the announcer, who sounded to Hank like he was performing in a radio drama. It was a little after 10 AM, and he'd been sitting down for maybe forty-five minutes. Hank had been in 1969 for maybe a couple hours after a mad dash to Atlanta in 2001, and the leadup to the countdown to the launch had been going on all this November morning.

He hadn't yet pulled the trigger on his decision to throw in the towel on all this time traveling. Every time he considered it, the clues became clearer to him, and the idea of the next port holding new answers was too tempting. Obsession was a poor travel companion, he supposed.

Hank wasn't alone. Some guy named Rodney sat across from him. They had met on the street, and his new friend Rodney seemed to have a way of inviting himself into Hank's life the way a tick invites itself onto a deer. So here they sat both eating.

The announcer stated once again that Apollo 11, the first mission to the Moon, had only launched back in July. Mankind, the radio voice declared, had made giant leaps so quickly in just a few months after millennia of development.

Let me tell you about time travel, you space cadets, Hank thought. *This will really blow your mind.*

Someone in the next booth asked Rodney for the pepper. He passed it over without the salt.

This is why we won't be friends, Rodney.

Rodney had a wispy mustache and curly brown hair over his shoulders. His linen shirt bore embroidered flower designs along the seams. The center of the flowers were stitched spirals. The jeans hidden under the table were bellbottomed, of course. The belt was braided rawhide tied over Rodney's fly like a shoelace or a bow.

"Meher Baba was the Avatar. He was my hero," Rodney said again. He added, "I wish I could reach back through the layers of time and touch him. Not just spiritually, but physically exist in his time on Earth again. To experience that time again, you know?"

It's not all it's cracked up to be, Rodney – being a time

traveler. Hank wondered if he would feel differently if he could remember who his family was and visit them. Not knowing who he was was one kind of torture. Going through all this knowing what you were missing and being unable to get back to it was another kind of torture, he supposed.

Was there anyone missing him in the future or in the past? Did it even matter? Apollo 12 was launching "today," but "today" was already history. 2025 was history. Hell, 3025 was history to someone in 4025. If Hank's home was somewhere along the timeline he had traveled, it was all set in stone and finished. Maybe it was already ordained that he never got back. If he did get back, every action had already been played out. He could hop through whatever barrier inhibited his future travel to 2999 and before the New Year celebration look up his history, his death date, his great great grandkids' death dates, and know the whole pointless story of his life. Maybe not knowing wasn't any worse than knowing. Maybe none of it mattered at all.

So, why all the dark SUVs and crazy clues? Having no point should be a lot less work.

Rodney was still talking. "I was actually in India at the beginning of the year. Baba wasn't doing public events anymore, but I had to see him. I was outside his house for weeks, but they wouldn't let me in to see him."

The announcer spoke under Rodney in the background. Apollo 12 was going to land in the Ocean of Storms. Hank assumed that was the name of a big crater or something. Music started up after that bit of Moon trivia that history was going to mostly forget. Hank sighed. The song was"Wedding Bell Blues" by The 5th Dimension. This was the third time today he had heard it. He had only been here part of a morning, too. Maybe it was a clue. He couldn't make himself listen to the words again, though.

Hank had picked up a few things from a news stand before Rodney introduced and attached himself. He had 3k in late 20th and early 21st century cash in his satchel, but only a handful of bills that passed in 1969. Now he had some change in the bottom of his pocket, too.

He got a Life magazine that sat wide on the table next to his greasy plate. One of the headline teasers was "Mailer on the Astronauts," whoever Mailer was. The man on the cover looked out at Hank with severe eyes. He had a sharp white crewcut and was taking a drag on a gnarly looking cigarette. He looked like he was thinking about kicking Hank's ass. That dude definitely would want to kick Rodney's ass, maybe the astronauts' asses too, by the look of him.

"So, he died on January 31st," Rodney continued after whining about all the time's he wasn't let in. "They put his withered body in an open box full of ice and flowers. He sat there for a week. There were thousands upon thousands of people there paying their respects. Almost turned the damn ice box right over. It was a riot. It was disgusting. I saw his body, the empty shell, but didn't get to see the man. Just disgusting. And unjust."

The other thing Hank bought was *The Andromeda Strain* by Michael Crichton. It had just come out in '69 apparently. Hank thought of it as an old book, but thought it was published in the 1980's. He could swear he read it before, but didn't remember any of it. If his memory kept betraying him, maybe he could just read it over and over forever and still enjoy it.

Port of Call by Brian Redd had just come out, too. Hank didn't get that one. It was a little too experimental for his tastes. Redd hadn't started using his middle initial at this point. If he ever met him, Hank would ask him why he started doing that.

Rodney said, "His last words were, 'Don't forget I am God.' Isn't that beautiful?"

Hank realized Rodney was waiting for an answer. "Um, I guess. If he really is God, I mean. Otherwise …"

Rodney's face contorted, but then went into a smile. "Otherwise, he might be like the psychos who painted crazy shit in blood all over Sharon Tate's walls, huh?"

"Right. Charles Manson calling himself Jesus Christ."

"Who?"

" … or Jim Jones … what?"

"Charles Manson?"

"Charles Manson, the guy who …" … *killed Sharon Tate. Oh, shit, have they not caught him yet?* Hank didn't remember the exact timeline. Jim Jones wasn't until the 70s maybe. Admitting knowledge to a mass murder weeks before it was solved might be bad. Before they happened might be even worse.

Hank cleared his throat. "He, um, recorded a song with the Beach Boys and then thought they weren't paying him enough. So, he went to the house and threatened to kill them. He lives on some ranch out in California with a bunch of women in this dangerous, violent cult."

"Sounds like a real winner," Rodney said.

"Yeah." Hank licked sweat off his upper lip. "No one worth remembering."

The house Manson went to when he wanted to confront one of the Beach Boys had already been bought by Sharon Tate. Hank had read this while browsing rabbit holes on the Internet one night recently – recently for him, but in future for the generation watching the Apollo landings. He needed to change the subject fast.

"Weird," Rodney said, "Who was the other guy you said? Jim somebody?"

"You were telling me about Meher Baba though," Hank reminded him.

"Right. Well, he's not like those guys. He was about peace and love and finding God in each of us. I stopped using drugs because of him."

Jim Jones got people off drugs, too, Hank thought, but kept his mouth shut about futures past. *Landing in the Ocean of Storms.*

"I went to Woodstock," Rodney said. "Peace and love and ideals, but drugs everywhere. It was a mess. They'll not discover anything, if they stay high all the time. The monsters who control the machines of industry stay sober, and they will march forward grinding over the travelers in their path while they are numbed by drugs."

I know the feeling, Rodney. Some of those masters of industry are drunk and on coke, though.

The waitress interrupted the hippie talk to refill coffee and offer pie. Hank declined, but Rodney said yes for both of them and offered to pay. Hank picked cherry, and Rodney called for a scoop of ice cream for both of them. Maybe being witnessed to by Rodney Baba was worth free pie. Maybe …

As Rodney paused to sip coffee, Hank stared out the window at paper Thanksgiving decorations in other windows. Was it already that time again? How many times had he lapped the mystic calendar of months without years? Kennedy was dead this Thanksgiving … both of them. Apollo happened partly because of his call to action. What if he could port through time to see how it all played out?

A movie poster advertised *A Bullet for Sadoval*. The returning cold made Hank's shoulder hurt where he had been shot in the early 20th. *You and me both, Sadoval old buddy … and the Dead Kennedys.*

The radio announcer kicked back in to drone about the Apollo launch some more.

" … deathless day …"

"What?" Hank pulled his eyes away from the window.

Rodney repeated, "I said, he told me January 31st will be called Deathless Day."

"Who told you?"

"Baba."

Hank shook his head. "I thought you said he died before you got a chance to talk to him."

"That's just it," Rodney said. "He's been visiting me in my dreams ever since the Deathless Day. He told me to be at Woodstock. To see and understand. He told me to be here to meet a lost traveler, trying not to be ground up in the gears of the machines. That's you."

Hank raised an eyebrow. "Really?"

The pie arrived, and Rodney went on while shoveling it into his mouth. "Baba taught us that the universe, the stuff we are made from before and after our lives here on Earth, is an eternal, shoreless ocean. It is forever wide, and it is forever deep, and it is all God. Each of us is a drop splashed up out of that ocean."

"An Ocean of Storms?" Hank asked. Pie and ice cream were better in the early 60s for some reason. It was even better than that in the 50s. Strange …

"Yeah, maybe." Rodney paused for a moment and went back to eating. "Each of us, as a piece of God, is meant to know ourselves in order to know God better."

Hank signaled for the check, and the waitress nodded.

"Baba was the Avatar, see? That word is Sanskrit for 'descent of God,' and he was God. We all are. Baba was the Avatar though. Before he was Baba, he was the

Buddha, Jesus, Muhammed, and many others, working to bring us to the truth."

Charles Manson … Jim Jones … Frank Edler … Hank would have been happy to trade all his random Internet knowledge about future cult leaders and killers for his own name and his own history.

"Men and women have chosen to be disconnected in time, drifting back and forth through it with no control," Rodney said. "We were meant to understand that time isn't linear. It cycles, but the years do not hold us bound within that cycle. They do not vanish when the cycle begins again. We can be free of that prison of time, if we find the doorways or the portals. We can control our passage back and forth between moments, if we stay sober and clean, and we stop letting forces and small men outside ourselves direct our journey by their narrow will and definitions. We are connected through this. We have a war to end. Without the prison of time, we might be able to stop the War before it even starts."

The waitress set the check on the table and refilled their coffees.

Hank blinked. "Wait. What did you say?"

Rodney smiled. "Which part, Hank?"

"The war that needs to be stopped. And controlling our passage through time. Small men controlling us. What does that mean? Which war?"

"Vietnam," Rodney said, as if Hank was an idiot. Maybe he was.

Hank said, "I need to get going."

Rodney picked up the check and held up his palm. "Wait here. I need to hit the head, and then I'll pay the check. Hold the table for us until I come back with the tip. I want to get one more shot of coffee before we head back into the world."

Caffeine is a drug too, Baba.

"Sure. I'll wait."

Rodney headed off. Hank waited until he was out of sight and started to gather his things.

His bag was gone. He looked under the table and all around. It wasn't there.

Hank looked toward the register. Rodney wasn't there, but he said he was going to the bathroom. So …

The announcer on the radio began the countdown.

Hank's eyes went wide, and he ran for the door. He pushed open the door to the diner with a ring from the bell.

"… nine … eight …"

A man behind the register shouted, "Hey, your friend already left. You need to pay before you go."

" … five … four …"

Rodney took everything. Hank needed to sprint before he got held and the cops came because he couldn't pay for pie.

He looked to the other corner of the restaurant in time to see Rodney's feet leave the ground.

"We have launched!" the radio announcer declared.

Savannah stepped into view around the corner

of the restaurant, as Rodney slammed to his back on the sidewalk. She had caught him across the throat in a clothesline strike. Then, Savannah yanked Hank's satchel out of Rodney's grasp. Rodney scrambled away from Savannah until he tumbled into the street. From there, he took to his feet and fled diagonally through the street empty-handed.

Peace and love, you jerk.

"Honey, I think you lost this." Savannah walked up to Hank and handed him back his bag. "Now, we're even."

"I did help you after you got stabbed, too, remember."

She rolled her eyes. "You want your bag and a medal?"

"Did you just appear here outside the restaurant?"

"I've been here a couple days. I was waiting outside because I spotted you, but saw you were with someone. I was about to leave, but then the guy ran out with your bag. Seemed like a great guy. Sorry it didn't work out. I hope you guys weren't getting close."

"Mister?" The man behind the counter put down his rag and started to come around to where Hank stood in the doorway.

Hank held up his bag. "Sorry. I was waiting on her. I'll pay the check. Savannah, you want pie? It's good with ice cream."

Chapter 15

November 20, 1969 - Apollo, Pennsylvania

Savannah had a gun, a hunting rifle. She was staring out the window of the farmhouse, toward the dirt road concealed in mist.

They'd traveled across the country via plane, everyone yammering about moon landings between sucking on their cigarettes. Hank made a witty comment about dying of second-hand smoke to a woman next to him. She didn't find it funny. He wondered if anyone even knew how awful smoking was for you in 1969.

He was here for the ride with Savannah. He'd slept with one eye open in a hotel room near Philly the previous night. When he'd woken, she was gone, but Hank knew she hadn't disappeared. Her satchel was missing, but she'd left a few personal items in the bathroom.

When she'd returned, she had motioned for him to be silent. She'd looked agitated. Hank had followed Savannah to the back parking lot of the hotel, where she'd produced a set of car keys and they'd climbed into a new Plymouth Roadrunner. New for 1969, anyway.

Hank hadn't bother to ask whether she'd stolen it or bought it with properly dated money.

"We're being followed," Savannah had said. "Someone was at our door this morning. Listening to us."

Hank had sighed and motioned toward the back of the car in the direction of the hotel they'd fled. "We were sleeping."

"I got up to go to the bathroom and saw the shadow. They ran down the hall when I started to unlock the door." She'd glanced from the road to Hank and frowned. "Have you been followed?"

"By you," he'd said and nothing more. He closed his eyes and feigned sleep. "Wake me at the next stop."

"It's close. Maybe four hours. Right near Pittsburgh."

Hank had wanted to ask her more questions, but he didn't trust her. He'd been conflicted with everything other people had told him. People he also didn't really trust.

Am I in this alone? What if part of this cosmic test is finally realizing I had to do it all myself, Hank had thought.

Savannah had skirted around Pittsburgh, taking a longer route than necessary. She'd spent more time glancing in the rearview mirrors than on the road ahead.

"No stops," she'd said. "I mean it."

Hank hadn't asked to stop. He'd been too busy trying to figure out all the scant facts in his head, circling back to the most important right then: was Savannah friend or foe?

When they'd arrived at their destination, a desolate farmhouse in the middle of nowhere, Savannah had parked the car inside the open barn and closed the doors.

She'd gone right for the flowerpot on the far left of the wraparound porch and had the front door key. When she'd opened the door, Hank had expected the inside to be empty or everything covered in sheets, but it was clean and pleasant.

Savannah had locked the door and pocketed the key. When she went to the nearest closet and took out two rifles, Hank knew she'd either been here before or owned the property.

"Which one do you want?" Savannah had asked Hank, holding out both weapons.

He wanted neither, but the thought of her armed, while he had nothing, scared him. He took the one on his left for no other reason than she seemed to be favoring the other one. Maybe that was going to be a mistake. Hank knew he'd only use it in self-defense, and it had better be a really good reason.

As she stood at the window with her hunting rifle, Hank's mind finished tracing the path of their most recent encounter back to the present, if 1969 could be considered the present. His musings about stepping off the loop of ports to live somewhere permanently was both tempting and terrifying. If he was being chased by someone, staying in one place and time felt like being trapped, just trading one time trap for another.

I'll never be free.

He tried to shake off these thoughts that spiraled down into deeper despair.

"You know this place," Hank said. He spotted a bent nail laying on the floor. He picked it up and set it on a table. It left a brown stain marking its shape on the floor.

"Get some sleep. I'll wake you at first light." Savannah motioned toward the open bedroom. "If you hear any noise come out shooting."

Hank opened his mouth to talk, but she put a hand up. "Sleep. Tomorrow we talk."

He'd slept well, despite the danger he knew was coming back, but had no idea what it was. The bedroom was small with no windows, a guest room with everything covered in a thin layer of dust.

His night went quickly with no dreams, no noises, and no shooting.

Come morning, she was still at the window.

"I made coffee. Keep the lights off," Savannah said from her spot. "Please bring me a cup. I think there are granola bars in the cabinet above the coffeemaker."

Hank poured two cups of coffee. In the fridge, there

was nothing, but he found nondairy creamer and sugar packets in the cabinet, but no granola bars.

When he emerged into the living room, Savannah was staring at him.

"No granola bars," Hank said.

She went back to looking out the window. "Maybe I ate them already. Maybe I never bought them in the first place. Yes, this is my home. One of many. I've only come here four times I can remember. There are plastic tubs of cash, weapons, and food all over the property. The attic is filled with boxes, too. Down the road is a pond. A family lives there. I pay them to maintain the property. Once a week the woman will come in and clean. Sometimes I leave notes for them. They never touch my things unless it's in a note."

Hank nodded and handed her a cup of coffee.

"There was no note even though I was here in 1967 and left one. They never move the notes so I know if something is wrong." Savannah turned to Hank. "Something is very wrong."

"Then, why are we here?"

Savannah shook her head. "I don't know. The clues I received clearly pointed to here, and when I saw you… I thought it all made sense."

Hank took a sip of coffee. "Can I trust you?"

Savannah smiled. "You don't trust me?"

"No," Hank admitted. "Not fully. Not nearly as much as I want to. Put yourself in my shoes. Would you?"

"Hell no." Savannah leaned the rifle against the wall and sipped her coffee. "Breakfast would've been nice. Not stopping for supplies was a stupid mistake."

"Let's order a pizza," Hank said with a laugh. He didn't know when pizza delivery had become standard, but guessed it wasn't in 1969. "What if you ring the caretakers and see if they have anything? It seems like you're paying them a good chunk of change. I'd be happy to give a few bucks for some eggs and bacon. Definitely toast."

"I'll go see them," Savannah said and stood.

"Let's go."

Savannah shook her head. "You can't come with me. You need to stay and watch the road. It's only a matter of time before they arrive, and if we're down at their home, we put them in danger, as well as don't have a chance to see them coming."

This sounds like a lie and not a very good one.

Hank sighed. "You want me to sit here while you do God knows what... I admitted I didn't trust you."

"You have no choice," Savannah said. She put her hands up, the rifle still against the wall. "If you have any doubt, shoot me. I'm serious. Kill me now. I told you about the money and weapons here. Take all of it. I don't care. The only way we can win is if we stay together."

Was this a trick, too?

"I'm having a hard time believing anyone I meet lately. It used to be simple. Find clues and move on to the next port. Now I think all the clues are fake, and I'm being led in the wrong direction on purpose. Maybe I was close to being out of this loop a long time ago, but being led in a huge circle means I'll never escape." Hank aimed the rifle at Savannah. "Maybe killing you gets me out of this."

"Maybe."

Hank knew he couldn't pull the trigger. While he didn't exactly believe everything Savannah was telling him, and he knew she was playing him to a certain extent, it wasn't in his makeup to kill someone in cold blood.

"Kill me or let me walk out the door," Savannah said and started moving, her back to Hank. "If you see a car or anyone, fire a shot. It will let me know they're here."

"Then what? They'll know where I am."

Savannah opened the front door, but stopped before leaving. "If you get into any trouble and we're split up again, I'll meet you on the twenty-first at 88 Verona Avenue in Newark, New Jersey."

"And if you're not there on the twenty-first?" Hank asked.

"Then, take what you find in the basement. It's all yours." Savannah glanced back at Hank and walked out into the mist. "Give me fifteen minutes."

Hank watched her go around the side of the house before closing and locking the door.

He took a seat where she'd been watching out the

window.

What was in Newark? Was it another safe house? Savannah's storage facility, like he had in New York City? She said hers was in New York, too. Hank hoped she'd be back so he could question her.

His stomach growled, and he drank the rest of his coffee, now getting cold.

Maybe when she returned, they could leave and go to Newark today. He was starting to get antsy and getting a bad vibe about this house. He wanted to leave 1969 more than he wanted to be free.

Hank was staring at Savannah's rifle still propped against the wall.

She'd forgotten to take it while they'd talked, and Hank hadn't even thought about it.

Savannah was out there unarmed.

Hank started to grab her rifle and try to find her. It wasn't safe, especially in this mist.

He heard a low rumbling outside and pressed his face against the window.

There were three black vehicles that appeared from out of the mist, single-file and coming fast down the dirt road. Not the same make or model as the ones in 1984, but maybe the closest 1969 equivalents.

Hank rushed to the front door and threw it open.

How long had Savannah been gone? No more than twenty minutes.

If they stopped, he'd have to fire at them, keeping the vehicles and their occupants at bay. Maybe it would give Savannah enough time to escape.

When it was obvious they weren't stopping at the house, and had veered to the left, Hank decided to take control of the situation.

Or, at least, create some chaos and let Savannah know they were coming.

Hank aimed at the lead car, hoping he could hit the front tire.

With any luck, he'd stop them. Get them to come after him.

Hank pulled the trigger.

Nothing happened.

He pulled it again and again with no luck.

"Dammit." Hank checked the rifle. There was no ammo.

Savannah had given him an empty rifle.

He turned and ran back inside to grab her weapon, which he found was loaded.

By the time he got back outside, the vehicles were long gone.

Hank ran around the house, but the mist that had clung to this place for two days now had swallowed everything past twenty feet.

"No. No." Hank ran down the dirt path, angling to the dirt road the cars had used and kicked up fresh dirt and mud.

Hank stopped short when he heard the first gunshot.

Savannah had left without taking her rifle.

Two more gunshots rang out in the mist, and Hank heard birds taking flight, wings flapping.

He ran back to the house and locked the door. Searched for more ammo. Found six more rifles and enough ammo to fight a war, along with clothes and jugs of water.

Hank heard vehicles coming closer. He took up position in the front window, setting extra rifles and ammo at the different windows.

The vehicles passed by at a high rate of speed and disappeared the way they'd come in.

No. Not all. One of them was missing.

Hank went out to the vehicle in the barn like each step might be his last. Someone could be a few feet away and hidden in the swirling fog.

He sighed in relief when the driver's door was unlocked and he saw the keys were still in the ignition.

Hank started the Roadrunner and drove away from the house, hoping he'd see Savannah again.

Chapter 16

November 21st, 1969 - Newark, New Jersey

"How many people are being born, and how many are dying today?" Hank asked out loud, as the dead man bled into the thick carpet.

Part of him expected time to unravel. Who the hell was this guy? Was he supposed to live another forty or fifty years? Was he going to have kids and grandkids?

Hank took three more breaths. He tried to make them deep, but they came ragged, on the edge of hyperventilating and hysteria. His brain misfired, and he couldn't tell if he was disappearing from existence, porting into oblivion without a room 138, or just passing out from shock.

He fell to his knees, still firmly in 1969, and was almost disappointed to still be alive and in existence.

The carpet was so thick and soft, he thought he might even be able to go to sleep on it, even with the body bleeding out into the grooves between fibers of the industrial sculptured touch carpet in white with pastel accents. Hank had no idea why he knew or thought he knew that detail. He was exhausted from the brief struggle and the terror.

Had he ever killed anyone before? He couldn't remember. How many times had the gun gone off? Was there anyone else in the building or outside who heard?

Hank's ears rung with loud deafness. He wasn't sure he could hear approaching sirens or footsteps anymore.

He realized he still held the sawed-off shotgun in his lap, clutched in both hands. With the same raw panic he would have used with a snake, Hank slapped and pawed the weapon away from himself. Once it rested on his shins below his knees, he could feel the heat from the barrel through the denim, and he kicked it away from him. The gun came to rest just past the soles of his shoes with the snubbed bores pointed between his legs at his crotch. Hank actually had to wait a few more ragged breaths before he realized it wasn't going to fire and bite him on its own.

It wasn't even his gun. He had tossed the rifle he had taken from Savannah's house along the highway on the way here. He wasn't comfortable with it anyway, and three police cars that looked like the old Ghostbusters' station wagons had raced by him on a hairpin curve along a two-lane road somewhere near the New Jersey border. Their sirens were out of time with one another and tones seemed distorted and off from what his brain told him police sirens should sound like.

Hank had nearly ran the stolen Roadrunner into the side of the last wagon, but then over compensated and ran off the road. His tires had ripped muddy tracks through the thick grass and slid to a sideways halt inches short of dumping into the creek. Despite the danger he knew he was in, he had pitched the rifle into the creek and started driving again.

As he'd continued up the road and into New Jersey, he debated whether police would find a rifle in a vehicle in 1969 unusual at all. He doubted they could run plates yet, but he didn't have a license or papers for what he was driving.

He still felt better without the gun, right up until he had to dive behind a stack of folded tables to avoid having his belly opened up by both barrels of the sawed-off shotgun as he entered the backdoor of the Verona Chemical Storage Annex at 88 Verona Avenue Newark, New Jersey.

Hank still wasn't sure how he'd seen and identified the threat in time to react. Sitting there alive seemed so unlikely.

The front door had been locked, and all the lights were out. So, he had walked around to the back, and it had opened to where someone waited.

The double blast had roared off with all the sound in the world, and Hank hadn't heard much else clearly since. A few pellets had managed to bounce through between the tables into his shoulder. He had waited for what felt like forever in the high hum of his damaged hearing. No new shot. No one came around.

He had decided to break for the door. As he rose, feeling like he was moving through water in a dream, he'd realized it must have only been a few seconds since the first blast, because the guy with long hair, a dark close-trimmed beard, and black sunglasses had only just broken open the sawed-off and thumbed in the first of two red cylinder shotshells.

The shotgun had closer than the door, so Hank had bounded over the top of the tables to the chewed up side of the stack, but hadn't reach the man until the gun was recharged and locked into place.

They'd struggled for it. The man had headbutted Hank twice, spraying dark stars across his vision and shattered his own glasses. The man had stunning blue eyes as the frames fell away into a stack of plastic buckets.

The man had walked Hank backward as they fought. He'd thrown knees into Hank's thighs, numbing Hank's muscles and sapping his strength. Hank had sunk his teeth into the guy's cheek, and the gun went off again, while the man had screamed in Hank's ear. They'd stumbled away from each other, him from the impact and Hank from confusion on who had been shot.

With the shotgun still pointing at him on the floor, Hank blinked several times, trying to keep the memory of all that violence from rolling through his head over and over again.

Splintered wood revealed the cheap particle board

interior of the tables to the right of where he leaned. The bite mark on the dead man's cheek stood out like an accusation. Three spent shells lay on the carpet a few feet back beyond the spreading blood.

Why have carpet this nice in a storage building only to have it ruined by blood in a shotgun fight?

The shells splayed open in a way that reminded Hank of cartoons. The man's chest caved deep into the body cavity on the left side where the flow of blood tapered off. Sections of two rib bones showed through. Nothing cartoonish there. Hank thought he could see the shredded heart inside the gaping wound.

I thought killing wasn't in my nature.

Bile crawled up from his gut, but he made no move to keep from vomiting all over himself. He felt like he almost needed it. If he couldn't vanish from existence, he needed to expel something. The poisoned feelings inside him had to get out of him somehow.

As he waited to be sick, he counted the shells. It came up three every time. His eyes lighted on the gun again. It pointed at his groin with one hammer still locked back. Hank forgot getting sick and forgot being exhausted. He scrambled to his feet and tracked through the blood past the spent shells to the opposite side of the room.

Now he saw the path of one red foot to where he stood pressed into the corner, and he couldn't stop thinking about a poem about Jesus leaving footprints in sand.

On the floor beside a double row of leaning metal folding chairs, Hank had to stare to understand what he saw on the floor. A box half filled with more shotshells made sense. A thermos with a red plaid print on the outside made sense. The unrolled sleeping bag could make sense too, if the guy was lying in wait long enough. The three satchels each with 138 pins did not.

He walked toward them leaving half a set of bloody footprints in the carpet. Hank opened each satchel with the same level of dread he harbored for the gun. All of them were empty though.

Hunting us …

If it had been one bag, empty or not, Hank would have thought he killed another time traveler like himself and Savannah. Three though had to mean something else. Trophies? Like time traveler heads on the wall? Had Savannah sent him here to be killed? Seemed like more work than just shooting him in his sleep. Right? She seemed like a no nonsense type. If there was murder to be done, do it the easiest way possible. Unless she answered to someone else.

There's a dead man in this room with you. Think faster!

Was this man here for both of them? He should have been harder to kill, if Hank was going to be his fourth trophy. Maybe if there was something other than coffee in the thermos he might have been slower than usual.

Did one of these bags belong to Savannah? That gave him pause. He had been half-heartedly ready to shoot her himself. There was no evidence in the carpet of previous target practice. She wouldn't have gotten here before him the way he tore up the road to get here, even if she had survived whatever happened at the neighbor's house and left soon after. She wouldn't have come in unarmed either.

"What is happening?" Hank whispered to himself and swallowed down a bitter taste in the back of his throat..

If I don't show up, use what's in the basement. That's what she said.

Through the rest of the building, he struggled with the piles of debris and with finding light switches until he finally found a set of stairs leading down into darkness. As Hank listened to his own breathing, more inside his skull than through his muffled ears, he considered what might be in the darkness waiting. The bloody track he left through the storage annex had shrunk from a footprint to light spotting.

Hank took the steps down, running his hand along the wall, feeling for a switch. He reached the basement with no light and no sense of proportion for the room. Along the walls, he impacted metal shelves and stacks of boxes, cracking his knuckles and stinging his knees. Still no switch though. Maybe he needed to go back to the stairs and feel along the other wall.

Then, his eyes adjusted enough to see the dullest glow from a dying security light to his right near one of the walls. There was a door within that weak spill of illumination. On the door … 138. Of course. It was written in marker or thin paint lines. It looked like the horror movie version of numbering rooms.

"Is this from her or from something else?" Hank's voice didn't seem to carry naturally through the air, but, of course, he thought he might have permanent hearing damage.

But why would she mark her own closet that way? Was this building something else she owned before, but it had gotten taken over when she missed rent for a couple years? The thing he was supposed to be looking for in the basement might be gone, too. His head was in no space to be processing new clues. He knew that no matter what happened, he was going to open that door before he left.

Hank left the wall behind and shuffled through the room toward the door. He scattered more plastic buckets and had to kick his way through the spill to get around. He stumbled and bruised his shins on more stacks, navigating blindly.

There were more letters – smaller – underneath the scrawled numbers. He squinted as he drew near, but then struck his knee hard enough to open wild waves of dizziness. The spots didn't clear, but grew into sparks of light. He felt himself falling, but couldn't tell which direction.

The 138 was scribbled out. No, not scribbling. Drawn over with a black spiral from a dying marker. The lines grew duller under the security light as they spiraled farther out.

The letters under 138: *The Clocksmiths will not allow.*

Even as he felt himself blacking out, Hank tried to

read them again.

Won't allow what?

The room exploded with all the sound in the world. There was more light coming from different directions in different colors. Hank realized he was still standing. The roar of sound was music this time with electric guitar, drums, and high vocals. As Hank became solid from the errant port, he felt bodies bump him from every side. His right shoulder shivered with pain from the embedded pellets.

It was the same damn shoulder he'd been shot in before.

Just grazed … You're tougher than all that, Sam.

The room was packed with people at a concert.

He tried to clear his head to understand where he was. This wall of sound hurt his head more than the shotgun blasts had. His instincts told him he was still in the same place, but something had changed. The door marked 138 was gone and everything else that had filled the room in 1969 had been erased. The year, that was what changed. 88 Verona Avenue did not look like the same building anymore, but he had been navigating in the dark.

He clutched his bag and worked his way through the crowd looking for a way out.

Chapter 17

November 22, 1988 - Newark, New Jersey

His ears were popping with the noise of the band onstage. After the shotgun blasts and everything else that had happened, he didn't know which was better: the absence of noise or this sonic assault.

The crowd was spread out across the large main room. Hank needed to look closer to see if it was a female with giant hair and makeup wearing tight animal-print leather pants and open shirt or a male wearing the exact same outfit.

Hank began weaving in and out of the small groups of fans, which had all eyes on the stage.

The band was dressed exactly like the crowd, with the long-haired pretty singer shouting for the crowd to sing along with him.

Hank thought they were covering a Cheap Trick song, a band from the 1970's that had obviously come back in vogue in 1988 for some reason.

How do I even know this is Cheap Trick? It's not even one of their hits, Hank thought. Obviously at some point he'd become a fan or had been before everything happened to him. Did it mean he was born in the 70s or 80s?

Hank sang along to the song, *He's A Whore*, knowing it was at least ten years old.

The place was now called Studio One. Hank had never heard of it, but he hadn't been in this part of New Jersey as far as he knew.

So many things I don't remember, he thought, making his way to the doors. He wanted to explore the building to see why it was so important, and maybe find what Savannah wanted him to do, and why she'd sent him here.

He got through the downstairs, passing another group of males and females dressed alike in their heavy metal uniforms and mullets, and got to the main floor.

There was a bar, currently packed and three-deep with those trying to get an overpriced drink.

Hank went outside for some fresh air and to get his bearings.

The line outside was down the block. More of the same metal fans, some staring at him because his hair wasn't long, and he wasn't dressed in a concert t-shirt.

It was dark outside and felt like rain.

Hank was hungry. Maybe he'd take a quick walk around the block and get a burger or sandwich. He got half a block away before he heard someone walking quickly from behind. Hank turned, stepping to the side, ready to punch someone who came too close.

"Newark at night in 1988 is a dangerous place. Hank, right?"

It was a dwarf.

No… it was *the* dwarf. The one Hank had seen before. The one he'd been warned about. Apparently, this guy was a time traveler, too. He had to be, but he didn't have a 138 satchel on him. Was he part of the group hunting them?

"You should go back inside Studio One." The dwarf smiled and offered a pudgy hand. "I'm Andrew. Friends call me Andy. Come on. I'll buy you a drink. I know the owner." The dwarf winked. "Savannah owns the building."

Hank hesitated. He could run away, attack the dwarf, or go with him.

"You coming? The headliner isn't here yet, and I know where their dressing room is. They probably have a ton of great food on their rider," Andrew said.

"Rider?"

Andrew was still walking away, back toward Studio One. "A list of the food and drink they want for the show. Specific kinds of beer or whiskey. Snickers or M&M's. Ever hear the story about Van Halen?"

Hank found himself jogging to catch up. "No."

"Brown M&M's," Andrew said and waved at the guy guarding the door and not letting anyone in line into Studio One.

Hank followed close behind and past the bar area to a hidden set of stairs, where they took three flights up and entered a large room. By the sound, they were above the stage.

Andrew spread his hands and smiled. "Help yourself before the band arrives."

"Won't they be mad if stuff isn't here like it's supposed to be on the, uh…"

"Rider." Andrew grabbed two cans of beer from a cooler, but kept them for himself, sitting on a couch. "Back to my Van Halen story. They demanded the brown M&M's taken out. If their lead singer, David Lee Roth, went backstage and saw brown M&M's in the bowl he'd trash the room. Destroy everything."

Hank shook his head. "Why?"

"It was widely reported they did it for the excuse to be mad and trash the dressing room." Andrew sucked down a beer and crushed the can in his small hand, tossing it on the floor and opening the second. "But there was a more practical excuse."

Hank picked up the discarded beer can and put it on the table near the cooler. He eyed a bag of unopened potato chips but decided against opening it, even though he was hungry. They were "sea salt" flavored whatever the hell that meant.

Andrew laughed, pounded the beer, and tossed the can over Hank's head. "Stop trying to be such a goody two shoes, Hank. It's totally unbecoming… and opposite of who you really are."

Hank had turned to pick up the can, but stopped and looked back. "You know who I really am?"

I killed a man downstairs.

"As I was saying… the real reason they specified no brown M&M's was so that they knew the promoter and his crew had read the entire rider. It wasn't really about M&M's; it was about knowing the gear was going to fit in the building. At the time, many tours had maybe three trucks of lights, gear, and pyro. Van Halen had nine. It weighed a ton. I believe literally a few tons. If something went wrong onstage, someone could get hurt. A lighting rig might collapse. At one concert the stage sank into the new flooring and cost tens of thousands of dollars."

Hank shook his head. "I asked you a question."

"Get me two more beers, and I'll get to the point of telling you this story." Andrew pointed at the cooler. "Hurry. The band will be arriving soon. We probably shouldn't be in the dressing room, even though we both know the owner."

Hank had too many questions. He bit his lip, not wanting to start asking about Savannah. Time traveler know-it-alls were long-winded.

"No beer... no answers," the dwarf said.

Hank got him two beers.

"You need to pay attention, something you haven't done yet or you would've figured this all out already." Andrew cracked open both beers. "Now… where was

I?"

"Telling me who I was."

Andrew laughed and took a small sip of beer. "Nice try, kid."

"Something about Van Halen."

"Oh, yeah," Andrew said and took another sip. "The point of my story is simple: pay attention to the smallest detail. It will save your life. It's why this is all happening."

"You could've just said that and saved your story."

Andrew shrugged and stood. "It's a cool story."

"Now tell me who I am, and what you know about me," Hank said.

"For starters, your name isn't Hank."

Hank shook his head. "I figured that. Tell me something I don't know."

"You were born in more than one place, more than one time, more than one person. Each time we complete a loop, really complete it, I mean, it buys the world more time. How? I got no idea. I'm only here because of what you've done. You wouldn't believe how many more days you've bought the world. You wouldn't believe how many years of porting each of those days cost. Some people have started to notice. They don't understand it, and they don't like it. 2035 or bust now, though," the dwarf said. He grinned. "I see by the look on your face you have a comment."

"I've never ported past New Years Eve of 2034."

The dwarf shrugged. "That makes sense, because,

just before midnight, the world will end as we know it. Not in a massive earthquake or due to World War III or IV, but just because he was done with this experiment." The dwarf looked up at the ceiling. "Then the new Eden is formed in the devastation, in a new primordial ooze, and we begin anew. Or that's how it used to play before the 138s."

"138s?" Hank shook his head. "You expect me to believe God gets bored with mankind and decides to wipe it out on New Years Eve, and then somehow creates an updated mankind, which I'm a part of?"

"What does it take to be God? Create new people? Check. Give them missions to save the world? Check. Live separate from the rules of time, space, and death? Check. Save all of humanity from the consequences of death and destruction from their sins? Check again." The dwarf pointed at himself. "*We're* a part of a select few. Including Savannah. The great conductor at the end of the world works the switches, and we roll through time bringing about his will." The dwarf took another sip of beer. "Think of it this way: we're in a video game. What do you do at the start, before you get into the action? You create a player. God created dozens of players. First level. A few simple survival skills. Instead of having to create the new world from scratch, maybe he rested on the new seventh day. Or the new ten thousandth day."

"How could you know any of this?" Hank asked.

The dwarf smiled. "I know better than anyone what the Trainman is capable of. You still think in black and white, right and wrong. You're missing the big picture, Hank Smith. You've taken over a previous player's character, and now you get to do whatever you want with him. We all do. Each of us that becomes the version of the old players, ready for another round of saving the world."

"Why?"

The dwarf shrugged. "Because there's an answer at the end of all of this, one that only he knows. You see? I'm playing the game right along with you, Savannah and a dozen others. Maybe hundreds. But fewer each time one of us gets hunted down. Maybe everyone you encounter is a new version of you and the role you play. A 2.0, if you will. We move throughout, not only the places, but the times those places were set. We evolve. Leave our footprint wherever we go. Change things in minute details. Just enough to change the future. Maybe we're doing it so that New Years Eve 2034 is just another day, with many more to follow afterward." The dwarf finished the latest beer. "Maybe we're amassing invisible points in this game and whoever gets the most at the end is the winner." He narrowed his eyes. "The rest are the losers, and they're deleted from the game."

Hank wanted to argue with the dwarf. Poke holes in his theory, if it was indeed just a theory. How could he possibly know so much?

"It's not a Butterfly Effect; it's the reverse. You are one of many stabilizers. Your tiny actions add up to stretching out the timeline and pushing out the ending. Any time you get wise, you get scrambled, blocked, chunked, and tossed back out to monkey through time all over again. All us 138s are trying to solve a puzzle while stabilizing and stretching out the years. We don't avert wars anymore. We push them through time with random human particles, like you, like her, like all the 138s. Because it is buying them more time, pushing back the end of the world piece by piece, they think there is one key change in the past that will turn the war off entirely. If you guys bounce around enough, you'll finally trigger it. Some of you cause too much trouble in the system though, so the agents of chaos peppered throughout time and the landscape take it upon themselves to extract you with a few bullets, if you get my meaning. They really hate you Hank. The Clocksmiths. You don't remember all of it, but you have a tendency to really gum up the works. Your mind is a little too curious, even with all the missing pieces. Maybe because of them. You better watch your back because the timeline is full of people who want to … extract you from the system." The dwarf stood and chugged the last beer. He tossed the empties on the couch and pointed at the door. "I'm going to leave. You should wait here. Don't follow me."

"You expect me to listen to what you said and not ask questions or follow?"

The dwarf nodded. "Savannah is coming through the other door in about six minutes. Plenty of time for me to leave." He grinned. "We're not exactly on friendly terms, and I fear she'll kick me or worse. She knows more than she lets on, Hank Smith. Remember that."

"She says you killed Alice, her friend in … the past."

"I loved Alice. The way you love …" Andy shook his head. "Doesn't matter. I didn't kill Alice. I tried to save her. The Clocksmiths got her. I tried to save her. Savannah didn't remember who I was yet. Still doesn't. Alice tried to hop off the train, but didn't quite make it."

"The Clocksmiths control all this? Who are they?"

"No, Mr. Train controls all this," Andy said.

Mr. Train is God.

Andy continued, "The Clocksmiths think we serve evil. They're hunting us for what we do. Most evil is done by those who think they are the heroes, doing what has to be done. We're caught in the middle."

"Then we're just pawns in a chess match created by God or Mr. Train?"

The dwarf laughed. "Honestly… I have no idea. It's just a theory from the pieces I do remember. I don't even remember what God looks like, if I ever saw him. I could be way off. Maybe none of it means anything. What if this is all a dream? Chaos theory? Who can really say?"

Hank had a feeling the dwarf could really say if he wanted to. He was toying with Hank now.

Andy held up a hand, shaking his pudgy little fingers. "Five minutes to Savannah. Give her a kiss for me."

"I won't let you go," Hank said.

"You really don't have a choice. I'll kill you if you

try to stop me," The dwarf said. "I don't want to. I actually like you, Hank. Yet, if it came down to it, I'd take you out of the game. Probably gain bonus points for doing it since, for some reason as yet determined, you are vitally important to all this. I'd love to see you live to the end and what role you really play, if you don't mind. I have a feeling you've been doing this far longer than most of us. You recruited me."

The dwarf held up three fingers before rushing out the door and slamming it behind him.

An hour later, when the band entered the room and gave Hank dirty looks, he realized he'd been duped by the dwarf.

Savannah wasn't coming, and he still had no idea what he was supposed to find in the building. He went downstairs and did another search through the crowd and the rooms, hoping something would jump out at him and let him know he was on the right track.

Mr. Train's tracks.

Hank stepped back outside and sighed in frustration. He felt like he'd wasted the day. Had that been the dwarf's point? To feed him full of lies and keep him away from what he needed to find?

Without a clue where he needed to go, but knowing Newark in 1988 wasn't a safe place, Hank began walking down the street in search of the next clue.

Chapter 18

November 26th, 2019 - Greencastle, Pennsylvania

Hank tried to clear his head, but straddling the dead man at the bottom of the shallow grave was distracting. Why did he even bother digging it?

"Because he was going to do the same for me." Hank's voice sounded strange and unhinged in his own ears. He realized he was still panting, so he tried to slow down his breaths.

He tried to focus on the task at hand. The 2019 phone was weirdly big. There was a phase in history where screens started getting bigger again when people realized they could watch porn on them. It was inconvenient back when phones still had hard screens that stayed the same size all the time. Where did they even put them when they weren't watching porn on the go? Not only were the screens huge, but they broke so easily. The dead man's phone had three deep cracks across the face. Hank wasn't sure if it was broken before they fought or not. It was broken now, though.

Hank brushed off the pad of the guy's right thumb to try to unlock the phone. In the dark, he pressed the thumb to swipe. Nothing. Hank held the device closer to his face. There were no buttons. He felt a wave of panic. Hank thought these things had a single round button at the bottom. He tried to think ahead of the "twenty-teen" years to what preceded the projected interface screens. Had he been to 2019 before? *Think …*

Leaning over the body, Hank lifted open the eyelids and held the phone above the man's face. The light changed, and Hank turned it over to see the phone was unlocked. Maybe it was an iris scan. Maybe it was face recognition. Whatever it was, it worked.

He stepped out of the grave and knelt, facing away from the body in the woods, between the bloodied shovel and his dirt-smeared notebook. Hank scrolled through the addresses, text messages, and notes. Most were clipped and encoded, but there was enough for him to write down what he recognized. The locations he found were spread all over the country, but mostly east of the Mississippi.

An address in Salt Lake City stood out, too. There was a lot number listed as "Northern Nevada." Lot 51275. It meant nothing to him, but he jotted it down.

Acidic urgency bubbled up in his chest, gut, and bowels. It tingled like something electric. He was sure they could track the phones, whoever they were, and he felt certain they could track the black SUV sitting several yards away on the edge of the road outside these woods. They might not know their man had been taken out instead, or that Hank was in the phone, but they might be closing in on him at that very moment.

He flipped to another page in his notebook, tearing it at the bottom near the spine. Hank opened Facebook Messenger and found uncoded conversations. Some of it seemed benign, like this guy lived an ordinary life when he wasn't chasing forgetful time travelers.

Why didn't you travel in pairs or in a group this time? Hank wondered.

One conversation went on for endless messages on how to operate older versions of Windows and Excel. Another was four or five guys busting each other's balls for years' worth of messages. He jotted a couple dates, times, and locations down from that thread, but couldn't tell if these "bros" were more dark agents like the dead guy who tried to chase Hank into the woods to shoot him. The shovel was from the back of this guy's SUV. Hank had used it on the back of the guy's head to be sure he didn't get up again.

"Can they track the guns, too?" Hank whispered. He reached back, dug through his satchel, and threw the dead man's gun into the grave with him.

They have to be coming, he thought. *Almost here …*

Hank opened Google Calendar and scrolled. November had a cartoon drawing of people walking in the rain with umbrellas next to a fountain. December had a cartoon guy cross country skiing. There were doctor and dentist appointments in multiple states.

Hank copied the addresses and other details. Hank slid the screens up and down to read all the words around the cracks in the glass. He was sure he was going to slice his finger before this was over.

Email revealed a short note about a meeting marked important in Nashville in a few days. Other emails revealed dates and locations of "teams." Hank wrote down what he could. He began to think none of these notes would make a bit of sense to him in the morning.

He double circled the Nashville meeting and stared at it.

There were over thirty thousand emails. He didn't check any past the first page of results.

He opened pictures. It looked like this guy was hanging out with multiple women, but the same couple kids. Hank thought he looked like an asshole even when he was in colorful clothes and smiling in the sunlight. He supposed he was probably biased.

"Were you a dad?" he asked out loud. If the guy had answered, Hank probably would have died right on the spot.

He paused on a few photos and figured out how to use his fingertips to zoom in and out.

On a brick wall in one of the pictures someone had written in what looked like chalk: Beware the black hand of the Clocksmiths.

Carved into the side of a black SUV, in another picture, someone had left the message: The world ended in October 1962. We've been dead ever since and don't even know it.

How did anyone have time to key that much into the side of one of their vehicles?

The next photo was back and white and framed-in too far to have any context. The edges were dark like the picture required a flash in a dark space. He couldn't tell what the surface was or whether the message was chalk, paint, or carved. It read, "Draw a line between the stars and find the train tracks of infinity spiraling into oblivion. Mr. Train holds it all."

He stared a long time at that, but then swiped to the next picture.

Hank froze when he saw pictures of himself. Some were from this port. The guy was following him, or had gotten the pictures from teams who were. Other pictures were from recent ports in the past. Recent from his point of view, but some distant in the natural flow of time. Some looked like digital images, and others looked to be copies of film that would be available at those times.

A text came through in a notice at the top of the screen. It was from a name marked Big Red that had been mostly strings of numbers when Hank had opened that one earlier. This message read: You made a huge mistake. You need to run.

He opened the text thread. This was the first whole sentence written between these phones. Hank looked around the woods. Staring into the phone made the darkness around him near complete. He typed: Explain.

Three dots appeared. Disappeared. Appeared.

Then, gone for several seconds.

"Come on," Hank growled.

The message from the person on the other end, maybe a friend, maybe not appeared: You know what you did. You know they're coming. Why aren't you moving?

Hank dropped the phone on the ground and stood over it. He heaved for breath. The vapor from his mouth was underlit by the phone below him.

An additional text bubble the same color as the others appeared. He squatted to read: Don't take the vehicle. Disappear.

Hank's fingers hovered to type something back, but didn't move. Did they know they were talking to him or did they think they were talking to the dead man? If it was to the corpse, why not stick to the code? Was it a trap? If they could trap him, why not send more than one guy to bury him in the first place?

The phone made a different tone that startled Hank. The screen changed to an incoming video call from Skype. The picture was identical to the red and blue 138 button on his satchel. The username was Room138Port2035.

Hank clenched his fists. He heard brakes squeal and doors slam. There were voices and flashlight beams from the direction of the road. He kicked the phone into the grave. He left the body, the open grave, the gun, the phone with the incoming call, and the shovel, but stuffed his notebook and pen into his satchel.

Hank Smith ran blind and without caution through the trees deeper into the woods and deeper into the darkness.

Chapter 19

November 27th, 2019 – Atlanta, Georgia

He was running out of time.

This was one of the addresses, but the building was stripped. There were connections for equipment that would work for an office that had its own servers. It wasn't dirty like a place that had been abandoned for a long time. Whoever had been here had cleared out, though. They left nothing behind. No clues.

Hank had picked up on the clues that told him he was running out of time.

There was a room 138 not far from here that was his next port. To where? Well, he knew he had no control over that.

There was a meeting in Nashville, in 2019, Hank assumed, but he would soon be in some other year. Maybe he didn't want to crash a Clocksmiths' meeting or a board meeting with Mr. Train and his council of time traveling demons. After killing the man who intended to kill Hank, whoever was going to be there was likely to be very happy to end Hank Smith, the most irksome of 138ers, right on the spot.

He still wanted to see who was going to be in that room. He wanted to see them when they saw him. The guy they wanted to kill and bury in the backwoods of Pennsylvania just stepping in like he owned the place.

It would almost be worth dying.

To regain that much control over his situation would be worth a lot of risk to him.

But that wasn't going to happen. He had to port in about an hour. So, his time was up and 2019's evil train conductors' meeting was going to slip by as Hank finished up November in another year.

"Is it just an excuse?" His voice echoed back at him off the bare walls. *Do I believe I can't make a choice because it's true, or because it's programmed into me by people who do not care whether I live or die?*

Something didn't add up. The people who set the 138ers in motion, whatever their reasons, giving someone the power to travel through time, only to decide to kill them off for "causing too much trouble" made no sense.

If you have the power to initiate time travel, how could you not travel through time to stop them? Why would you count on gunmen and black SUVs? Lone men with text message codes and a shovel to bury a time traveler in Pennsylvania.

"Two different groups?" Even as he said it, Hank had no idea what it meant.

One group who wanted the 138ers doing what they were doing and another group trying to stop them might make more sense. But why do it this way? Why start amnesiacs flitting from year to year, just to follow clues to their next jumping off point? There was no purpose to it.

No purpose Hank could see, anyway.

One group doing this all or two groups working against each other, someone else was in control.

"I'm about done being controlled."

Hank took out a knife and started carving into the walls. Not deep, but enough to form his letters in jagged scars: Mr. Train is not my god.

He stared at it a moment. He carved again: I left your man in a grave he was going to dig for me.

Hank was done with being controlled, he decided.

In the end, he left the empty office and went to room 138, though. Because that was what the clues told him he was supposed to do.

Chapter 20

November 28th, 1975 – Chattanooga, Tennessee

It was probably the wrong year, but Hank went to check out another one of the addresses. The place was a split level ranch with painted brick and angled wood on the outside. It was for sale.

They were having an open house.

Hank stood outside and stared for a long time. Then, he went inside.

A woman in a burgundy and mustard colored short dress with long sleeves greeted him. Her hair stood tall and sculpted with purposeful curls framing her face.

She handed him a card. She was Alicia Nash of Music City Realty. They had offices in Nashville, Chattanooga, and Memphis.

She followed him over the shag carpet onto the linoleum of the kitchen as she was spouting off the features of the house. The place was furnished. He saw nothing that clued him in to any men from a secret society planning the deaths of time travelers.

"So, what are you looking for in a home, Mister …"

"Um, Smith, I'm … Shane Smith."

"Are you a bachelor?"

"No, I'm married. Moving down from … up north." Nothing in the bedrooms caught his attention either.

"Any children to fill up these bedrooms?"

Something clicked inside his head, but then he lost whatever it was.

Jesus, laying in on thick, Alicia Nash.

"Not yet, but we're hoping." Hank returned to the kitchen. He felt uneasy. Was it talking about family? Was it being here at all?

"It'll be a great house to start a family in."

It really kind of was, Hank thought. Of course, Savannah already had some places of her own scattered through time. And she might be trying to kill him either for Mr. Train, the Clocksmiths, or both.

Another couple walked in. They looked like better potential buyers. Alicia's eyes seemed to indicate she thought so, too. "I'll let you look around, and I'll check back with you."

Hank thought about children in the bedrooms. He could picture it, but it was a different place, in a different time.

"Saint Mary's," he whispered.

As soon as the words left his mouth, this strange

name, whatever it meant, was out of his reach. He thought about the flood in Louisiana he had ported into, that intense moment of fear of a storm. He remembered a nun he saw one Halloween. A nun who might work in a place called St. Mary's maybe? He had nothing. He didn't understand what any of these pieces meant.

He had his own storms to deal with here, maybe storms of his own making.

As she went to greet the other buyers, Hank pictured the Clocksmiths in their black SUVs using this as a base of operations in the future. Maybe one of them was going to buy it at this very open house or maybe another sale a couple decades down the timeline.

Hank stood here in the spot where those hunting him would one day make their plans.

What was the point of being a time traveler, if it didn't give you an edge over your enemies?

Alicia showed the couple the kitchen and then left Hank alone again as she showed them the bedrooms.

He took out his knife and opened one of the cabinets. He reached in and carved into the underside of one of the drawers: 138. I was here before you.

Hank left before they came back out of the bedroom.

Chapter 21

November 29th, 1975 - Nashville, Tennessee

He found another office that had been abandoned. Almost anyway. He was actually only two doors down from Music City Realtors' Nashville office. This address was unmarked, but also in the wrong year.

Hank found the photos though. They were in a folder that had slipped down behind an empty shelf. The edge of the manilla was just poking out in sight.

When he spilled the photos out on a table with no chairs around it, he saw murder scenes. He couldn't tell how many because more than one of the black and white photos showed the same room and bodies.

There were satchels and 138 buttons. He saw the faces, but didn't recognize any of the victims. One was a woman. One was a man. He couldn't tell if there were more than two scenes.

As Hank stared at the photos on the table, a guy entered the front room of the office from the back hallway even though Hank had searched the building and found it empty. He carried an empty cardboard box and wore a grey suit.

The guy stopped cold when he saw Hank.

Hank turned, and the guy stared at the 138 button. His eyes went wide. "Holy shit. You're really real."

He dropped his box and reached for the holster on his hip. Hank wanted to run for the door, but charged the man instead. The guy's holster was empty, and he got out half of a curse before Hank drove his forearm into the guy's throat and slammed him into the corner of the doorway.

The guy blinked, but then opened his eyes revealing one blue eye and one green eye.

"Who are you? Who do you work for?" Hank brought his open pocket knife up into view, and then held it to the man's throat.

"Relax, Mister. Relax."

"Answer my questions or I'll carve 138 into your fucking throat."

"I'm just hired to log data."

"Log data for who?"

"The FBI."

"What?" Hank eased back just a little, and that was his mistake.

The guy caught Hank under the chin with a tight punch and raked the knife out of his grip. Hank stumbled backward and tasted blood where he had bitten his tongue, but he didn't fall.

The guy went for the knife, and Hank ran for the front door.

"We got your picture," the man yelled at Hank's back. "We'll get you, too."

Hank charged up the sidewalk past the realty place and kept going.

As he laid down to port that night, he thought, *That asshole didn't work for the FBI. Either he was lying or the people who hired him were lying. He didn't even keep chasing me.*

That still didn't put Hank much closer to figuring this all out.

His tongue hurt. His shoulder still hurt from being shot twice.

He fell asleep and woke up still in Nashville.

Chapter 22

November 30th, 2011 - Nashville, Tennessee

The bar wasn't to Hank's liking. Too new, but it tried to look ancient. The country music was the safe stuff you'd hear on any country music station, the big hits, the guys in cowboy hats who hung out with perfect white teeth and designer cowboy boots at the CMA Awards.

He had driven past the same office from 1975 after he ported to Nashville again in a different year. The Music City Realty location was a vape shop, and the Clocksmiths' office was a pet store. Maybe when Hank showed up right in their midst, they changed locations. He might have changed history, and now all the addresses from the dead man's phone were no good anymore.

That man didn't die until 2019, so maybe he was still walking around alive right now, hunting for Hank. If he found Hank and killed him in 2011, would that change things in 2019? They would literally kill and dispose of each other eight years apart.

If you're seeking revenge, dig two graves.

What was he seeking? Freedom? Control over his life and destiny? Answers to all of it?

Hank wasn't drunk enough for this line of thought.

The bar itself wasn't wood, just made to look like it with perfectly placed scratches and faux initials carved in it. The walls were fake wood and so was the floor.

Even the waitresses looked fake, with unnaturally large breasts and smiles.

"Care for another?" The bartender, a bored-looking pretty boy, asked, not even trying to do the fake Southern accent after the first greeting. He sounded more New York than Tennessee.

Hank had been nursing the same beer for an hour, and he had a sip or two left. He shook his head, and the bartender moved off to ask another drunk on the other side.

There were maybe six people in the place right now, although in an hour, once the dinner crowd was finished filling bellies with food, they'd fill the rest with overpriced beer.

A guy in a black leather jacket with long dark hair and a goatee walked in carrying a guitar case. To Hank, he looked out of place in Nashville. If he'd been wearing a bolo tie or a black cowboy hat, maybe he'd fit in.

Hank supposed he was new in town, and in a few weeks he'd blend in with the right garb and attitude, selling his rock and roll dreams for a country one.

The guy placed his guitar case against the bar a couple of stools down from Hank, but didn't look at him. "Shot and a beer," the guy said.

Hank finished the last sip of his. The place was getting crowded, and he wanted to be alone. He'd come to town and followed the cryptic clues in the phone of the man he killed, more damn signs just like always, but he just ended up in another bar. Unless he'd missed a connection, he was now stuck.

When he stood, the guy glanced in his direction and shook his head. "Let me buy you a beer, friend."

"Thanks, but I was just leaving." Hank took a step.

"There are two of them outside. One with a rifle. He'll blow the top of your head off before you can blink." The man smiled as the bartender put down his drinks. As soon as he walked away, the man raised his shot and saluted Hank. He downed it and smacked his lips. "Have another beer. We should talk."

"One time I'd like to sit down near someone, and they're just a normal person and nothing more," Hank said. He sat.

"I'm a normal person." The guy glanced at his guitar case. "Just a wandering musician. I play a bit of guitar here and there."

"Here and there?" Hank asked skeptically.

The man smiled and extended a hand. "Matt O'Leary. Pleased to meet you…"

"Hank. Shouldn't you already know this?"

Matt shrugged. "I know about as much as you do, Hank. I was on my way out of town when a mutual friend gave me a handful of cash and told me to come in and save your life."

"That didn't sound odd to you?"

Matt shook his head and took a sip of his beer. "Like I said, I wander and play my guitar. I make money any way I can, mostly the legal ways."

"You talked to Savannah?" Hank asked.

"Don't know who that is. I talked to a guy in a trenchcoat wearing a Fedora. Very dramatic. He spoke in hushed tones. Said he needed to protect you." Matt snapped his fingers. "Said you were an important asset to his business, whatever that means. Know what it means?"

Hank shook his head. "I thought you said a mutual friend asked you to help me."

Matt nodded with a smile. "I did. Money is a mutual friend."

"You port, too?"

"Wherever the muse takes me. You want another beer?"

Hank looked toward the front door. "Won't they get impatient and come inside?"

"I doubt it. They're getting paid by the hour." Matt grinned. "They're not like us. Just some hired thugs doing a job. If we close the place, they'll eventually walk off… or your benefactor will get rid of them."

"I thought you were here to save me?" Hank asked.

"Nah. I'm really here to babysit you. Make sure you don't walk out the door and get killed." Matt waved at the bartender for another shot and beer and motioned for another set for Hank. "The back door will probably be covered as well. As long as no one sketchy comes into the bar, we'll be fine."

Hank wondered how long they'd have to wait before he could leave. The idea of getting drunk in a bar, while a hired assassin was outside waiting to take a couple of inches off the top, wasn't what he had in mind.

There were three saltshakers on the bar next to where Hank sat. The bartender took away two of them.

"You got a band tonight?" Matt asked the bartender.

When the bartender shook his head, Matt smiled. "You do now. Mind if I get up onstage and jam a bit?"

The bartender shrugged. "They won't pay you, and there's really no one here."

Matt stood. "Then you won't mind at all."

"You'll still need to pay for the drinks, too."

"Of course." Matt took out a twenty and tossed it on the bar, winking at Hank. "You play an instrument?"

"Not that I'm aware of," Hank said. He took a sip of the beer and ignored the shot for now. "I was hoping your guitar case had an assault rifle inside so you could bust me out."

Matt put the case on the bar and opened it. "This, my good man, is a 1958 Gibson Les Paul in original condition. It goes for a lot of money. You won't hear a better sound from any instrument past or present. I wouldn't trade it for all the tea in China. I've had this baby with me for many years, and once I start playing, people stop and take notice. Why? Because I'm that good." Matt grinned and gently took the guitar out and adjusted the strap. He looked comfortable and relaxed with it on.

"There's a drum set," Matt said. "Wanna see if you can play?"

"I can't." Hank knew he wasn't musically inclined.

"Anyone can tap on a drumhead. It's not that hard, which is why the drummer never gets laid. All you got to do is keep time. You can keep time, Hank," Matt said and winked. "Let's kill some time."

"Poor choice of words." Hank followed Matt to the stage and sat on the drum stool. "There aren't any sticks."

"Drummers usually hide them under the amps." Matt began strumming his guitar, tuning it. "You know any songs?"

"I know a lot of them, but not to play one," Hank said. He got down onto the floor of the stage and felt underneath the amp. Sure enough, he pulled out a set of drumsticks.

"I'm more into the old country stuff. Johnny Cash. I don't think this crowd will want to hear Metallica or

Volbeat. We might get away with AC/DC." Matt put a mic stand in front of him. "Is there a mic I can use?" he asked the bartender, who shook his head.

"Then lucky for you my voice projects." Matt turned to Hank and grinned. "As long as I'm on a stage, I'm in my element. You ready?"

"No." Hank had no idea how to hold the sticks. How to play or keep a beat. He had no doubt he knew nothing about playing an instrument.

"You know the intro to *Highway To Hell*? That might be a cool one to get the crowd moving," Matt said.

Hank shook his head.

Matt seemed to be thinking. "Follow my lead. I know what we'll play."

When he began strumming the guitar, Hank had no idea what song it was.

Matt began strutting back and forth across the stage, his long hair flipping up and down to the rhythm of the music.

Even when Matt began to sing, and he had an amazing and strong voice, Hank knew he'd never heard the song before.

Hank decided to join in with the bass drum and try to figure out the beat.

It must've been good, because Matt nodded with a smile before singing again.

There were three women, all looking way too old for the skimpy outfits they were squeezed into, and a couple of the fake-hot waitresses, who were drawn to the front of the stage.

Hank decided to use the sticks to keep the beat, and he thought he was doing a manageable job. Matt didn't complain, and the women began to dance.

Hank started to enjoy himself, especially when Matt played songs he actually knew. While his drumming was amateur, and he couldn't figure out exactly how a song went, he did his best and felt like he'd only made a few mistakes.

After three hours of playing, in which time the bar filled up, Hank was getting a few sporadic cheers from the crowd. Most of the applause was for the job Matt was doing.

The guy seemed to know every song ever written and how to play it, and when someone yelled the name of a song he'd nod and start to play it.

Hank's arms felt like they were about to fall off.

"Let me chat with my drummer for a second," Matt said to the crowd.

As everyone cheered, Matt came to Hank. "You ever see *The Blues Brothers* movie?"

Hank nodded.

"In the movie they find a hidden trap door on the stage and sneak out using it," Matt said. "I'm going to play a few ballads. Guitar only. I appreciate you playing with me, and I hope you get wherever you're going and find whoever Savannah is." Matt extended a hand and Hank shook it.

"Wait… there's a secret door?"

"Right behind the drum kit. I'll distract them," Matt said.

"Why didn't we just leave then?"

Matt shrugged. "It's not often I get to jam with anyone new these days. Besides, they'll probably be gone by now. This way you can get across town through the tunnels and to safety. Safe travels, my drummer friend. Another time and place, maybe."

Chapter 23

December 3rd, 1944 - Gary, Indiana

He didn't remember the flashlight had even been invented yet until he found and stole one. Savannah would be so proud. Then, he tracked down this address from the information he had found in the phone of the man he killed years in the future. It was the wrong time, but he searched it anyway.

The moonlight through the windows wasn't enough, but he didn't like what the flashlight showed inside the factory. An array of symbols were scratched into the rust of the boilers and sheet metal walls. Spiral swirls, backward numbers, and interconnecting lines that looked like the tags for serial killers covered everything back here. The "138" in the middle bothered him the most.

Off to the side, looking like it might not be part of the rest of this, someone had scratched in: Mr. Train has his hand upon the switch BUT he doesn't know which way to flip.

Hank stared at that a long time. That was probably the key to everything, he thought, but he had no idea what to do with it. He copied it down in his notebook anyway.

Then, he saw a thing that stopped him cold. Carved into the rust of one of the tanks was: Draw a line between the stars and find the train tracks of infinity spiraling into oblivion. Mr. Train holds it all.

Was this where that picture in a dead man's phone was taken? A dead man who hasn't been born yet. There might be a man with one blue eye and one green eye who might have just been born, though.

Moving the flashlight up and down from the surfaces to his notebook where he tried to copy down all the symbols, gave him a headache. It also attracted the attention of the cops who had a flashlight or two of their own.

Hank squeezed himself into a dark corner and alcove. He made himself as small as he could in the cold darkness and waited.

"Yeah, a kid from Ohio State won it this year. Sounded like a damn Kraut name to me. Can you believe it?"

The light drew closer as it cut from side to side behind the boilers, throwing mad shadows.

"Stupid little trophy anyway. Who cares about college football? Hell, how can you follow it anymore, anyway? They're about to merge the Steelers with Chicago into one team. That bothers me more than any German college student cleaning up on the field."

"Pittsburg and the Cardinals on one team? What a world."

They stopped just on the other side of where Hank hid. He could hear their heels turning on the grit in the floor.

"Who do you even root for or against anymore, right?"

"Guess all the players and all the action is across the world. Can't even follow all the occupations, liberations, and setbacks anymore."

"Roosevelt's got himself a fourth term to bring the Reich to heel. We'll just keep reelecting him until he becomes a king or a New York savior, I guess."

"I'm not seeing any intruder or light in here. Are you?"

The light swept the ceiling. "Not a Jap fighter or Nazi bomber in sight. Looks like we kept Gary safe from the Hun devils another night."

They made their way out the front, taking their light and complaints with them.

Hank waited another twenty minutes before he couldn't take the cold anymore and crawled out of his hole. He dropped his notebook in the dark and then kicked it. Bits of gravel and broken glass bit into his palms as he swept his hands along the ground. Everything in him wanted to turn on the stolen light again, and everything feared it, too. His knuckles cracked against metal, sending hollow thuds echoing through the building and maybe out into the night.

He felt more discarded nails across the floor as he continued to search.

His fingertips grazed the corner of the pages under a suspended drum and spun the notebook. He brought his hand back and found the book's spine. Without shaking off the dirt and grunge from the factory floor, he shoved the notebook into his satchel before running through the building to the doors.

It was colder and windier outside, but so much easier to breathe again. The blackout darkness of the small town made the Milky Way a brilliant tapestry across the frozen sky. Hank tilted his face up into it and breathed mist from his lungs into the stars. In them, he saw the same spirals and backward numbers he had seen carved in the rust inside a building that somehow belonged to his enemies, his hunters, across time. He knew, if he stared long enough, he'd see 138 in the sky, too. He'd see more messages about what room came next, and what empty jump into another time would come after that. It was written in the stars, and carved into the walls all around him – one clue leading to another across time and through eternity. He'd see it whether it was really there or not because that was all he had left. All memory, family, life, and meaning were gone to make room for the clues.

Lights blazed on, washing out the stars and the entire Earth. "Stop there. Who are you?"

Hank ran from the spotlight and into the field behind the factory. The icy grass whipped at his pant legs and the solid snowfall broke under his heavy heels. He could hear them behind him, pursuing. They were always pursuing.

Chapter 24

December 12th, 2027 - Rusty Nail, Nevada

Room 138 was spacious, cold and uninspiring to Hank, with white walls and beige accents. He'd been able to check into the hotel without any human interaction, using the white plastic card he'd had in his satchel since the first time he remembered checking the contents. He knew in the past he'd dwelled on the card, wanting to understand what it was and what it was for. He'd forgotten it, marking his place with it, in an old book.

So, here was the great mystery.

Apparently, it was used in the future, although it had no numbers or words on it to study.

Hank had instinctively known it would open room 138 this time.

When he opened the large walk-in closet, he gasped. The three sides of the closet had hundreds of clothing items hanging, all wrapped in plastic. Starting from his left, they were outfits in his size and from different time periods. Hank knew, if he went through the lot, he'd go through time in clothing.

Hank felt like he'd been here before, too.

A couple of shoe racks held various pairs to match up with the outfits.

In the three dressers under the hanging clothes, he found watches, underwear, socks, hats and other items of dress.

He ran his finger over the nearest plastic and came away without any dust, but it could simply be that a robot or device in the room made sure nothing got dirty.

Hank checked the rest of the main area and found the other drawers of the three dressers filled with more of his clothes, packages of money marked in five-year increments, and six bottles of whiskey.

The other door across the room intrigued him. He opened it and sighed.

It was a mirror of his walk-in closet, but it was filled with women's clothing. All laid out in the same way his closet was.

He knew he shared this room 138 with Savannah.

Hank glanced at the one king bed in the room. Were they together in this future? Lovers?

It didn't sound likely. Hank believed, no matter what was happening between them, it wasn't physical. It had never been and would never be anything but a sort of friendship.

That's what he thought, as he stared at the king bed.

Hank didn't know if they were friends, though. If he believed the dwarf, they were all in this together. If he believed Savannah, the dwarf was the enemy. Andy, the beer-guzzling little person, claimed that was all a misunderstanding.

Alice tried to step off the train and failed.

This felt like a base of operations for them. He'd thought he only had the one storage unit, but, as he walked around the room, it was familiar. Maybe he'd spent a lot of time in *this* room 138, sometime before he forgot everything.

Maybe so had Savannah. What if they both used this location, but were never here at the same time? They respected one another's stuff, but had never actually shared the bed.

Hank wondered how many more there were just like this, in different places and times. Other 138ers doing their 138 thing.

In order for this to still be available, it meant they'd paid far in advance and who knew how far in the future. It might even be an automatic system where, each day or week or month, money was pulled from an account.

Maybe in the year 2027, it was taken from the white card and paid out. Hank knew he didn't need to worry about money, especially since he'd found so much of it in the drawers.

He felt tired, lonely, and lost as to what to do next.

The door opened, but if Hank hadn't been facing it, he would've never known, the door sliding open without a sound.

Savannah stood in the doorway, and she didn't look surprised to see him.

Hank gave her a smile, despite all his doubts, but she didn't return it, stepping inside. He couldn't figure out what the look on her face meant.

"We can't leave for two days. We lock the door and don't answer it no matter what," Savannah said.

"What about food?"

Savannah stepped back into the hallway and pushed a large box with her foot into the room. "I brought sandwiches and snacks, as well as bottled water. We'll be fine."

"Why are we staying in the room for two days?"

"I'll explain everything once we eat. I'm starving. I spent the last few days being chased by the natives in the area. Eating berries and drinking from a stream." Savannah closed the door.

Hank helped her unpack the food and drink, placing everything on top of one of the dressers. She had sandwiches in plastic bags, as well as potato chips.

"Is this from where we are now, or did you bring it with you?" Hank asked.

"The food was made in 2001, but it's still fresh, over twenty-five years later," Savannah said and laughed.

"How did you get it…"

She put up a hand and took a bite. "I told you, I

haven't eaten real food in a while."

Hank knew enough about porting to know her story made no sense, but he didn't want to push her. Besides, as soon as he took the first bite, he realized he was a lot hungrier than he thought he was.

They ate in silence, smiling and eating like it was their last meal.

Hank knew it very well could be.

When Savannah was done sharing a box of chocolate chip cookies with Hank, she gathered up the garbage and put it back in the box.

Hank had been sitting on the bed while Savannah was cross-legged on the floor. Now she joined him.

He felt his face flush when their legs touched as she got comfortable.

"Our next destination is Utah. I already have the clues," Savannah said. She shook her head. "The real clues. Not the ones spoon-fed to us to keep our paths going in an endless circle."

"Then you've solved this? We can figure out what's at the end of this journey?"

Savannah shrugged. "I'm not sure if there really is an end. We might be spinning our wheels for the next ten years. If we pass New Year's again …"

"What? What happens? What do you mean?"

She shook her head and looked away. "I don't know. I'm still figuring this out."

He stared at her a while and then asked, "Are we getting older?"

"I don't really know. It feels like our memories and bodies can only hold so much information. Do so much… before we're wiped clean and start over. A reset."

Hank sighed and fell onto the bed. "To what end? Why is this happening? What are we supposed to be looking for? Why the two of us? Why the others? Why the Clocksmiths?"

She sat up. "What do you know about them?"

He narrowed his eyes looking up at her. "What do *you* know about them?"

"They're trying to kill us," she said. "There's more of them in some time periods than others. I'm not sure what they think we're doing, but they want to stop us however they can."

"Are they the same people who started this?" Hank asked. "Mr. Train?"

"They don't seem to travel through time. They just know that we do."

"Do you know who Mr. Train is?"

She shook her head. "Tell me what you know."

Hank recounted his adventures since last seeing her. He realized he was sharing more than she was.

"So," he said finally, "it's just the two of us against the world, apparently."

Savannah slid closer to him on the bed and stared into Hank's eyes. "Don't you see… it's more than just the two of us. There might be dozens like us. Hundreds, even. How many have you met?"

"A few I can remember. Evidence that others have been hunted down by the Clocksmiths. Although now that you mention it, I feel like there might be a lot more in my past."

"Exactly. A past we've forgotten, or the memories wiped from our thoughts. We're being manipulated, and I think I know why," Savannah said. She sat up. "But we need to keep moving forward before I can say with certainty why we're doing what we're doing. Behaving like lab rats. Going through the motions."

"What if you're wrong, and we're trapped in one time?"

Or we die trying to hop off the train?

Savannah fell back on the bed and groaned. "I don't have all the answers. I might not have any, in fact. I just have a gut feeling that I've been trying to deny. A fear, in fact."

Hank understood. He had felt the same thing. "What if, by getting too close to the truth, our memories are erased?"

She nodded slowly, her eyes staring past him. "That would make sense, although if one of us got too close and had a reset, wouldn't the others still know?"

"Maybe the entire system resets," Hank said. "That way no one can get close to the truth." He shook his head. He knew he was on to something, but that simplistic theory had way too many holes in it. He knew it was wrong. "It seems like everyone I run into knows way more than I do. Including you."

"I don't," Savannah said, but Hank didn't believe her. He'd gotten away from her once before. Would he need to do it again? He was so conflicted. Was she here to help them solve this, or to keep Hank in an endless loop of ports?

"Did you text me through that Clocksmith's phone to warn me? Was it you?"

She shook her head. "I wouldn't even know how?"

He chewed at the inside of his mouth. "This would make more sense if we were programmed to kill or do a definite task."

"You mean like kill Hitler or make sure Jesus wasn't nailed to the cross? The big stuff?" Savannah asked.

Hank nodded.

"Sounds like you're killing just fine, Hank. Two since I last saw you."

He closed his eyes and sighed. "Both of them were trying to kill me. I had no choice."

"So much for small footprints," she said. "What if we're unwittingly changing things just by being in certain places at certain times? Maybe even small things. Not just killing Clocksmiths."

Hank smiled, "I thought you didn't believe in the Butterfly Effect. You chewed me out when I first brought it up."

Savannah shrugged. "But what if it was a thing? Maybe a thing if some figure like Mr. Train knew exactly when and where to send us?"

"Could something like this ever be orchestrated?

Where would this godlike figure sit as he watched the changes we made to time while he flipped the switches?" Hank sat up. "You think this is a game being played using us?"

"I don't know." Savannah shook her head. "We're only guessing at this point. We could be so far off."

"What does your gut say?" Hank asked.

Savannah closed her eyes. She frowned and blew out air, shaking her head. "I don't know. I can't explain what I feel. This is terrible."

"I feel like we're onto something monumental, but I don't know what it is." Hank felt as frustrated as Savannah seemed to be. "What do we do now?"

Savannah opened her eyes. "We wait. My gut is telling me that. We don't do anything until it's time to make the next port."

Chapter 25

December 15th, 1985 - Salt Lake City, Utah

Something wasn't right. They walked down the center of the street, Hank on the right, Savannah on the left. No cars moved. No people walked around. They hadn't seen a soul since yesterday, the day after they ported into the city.

They had the date right. TV, news, radio, the cars, the styles of clothes all fit the year, but now the place was barren, and they knew of no historical explanation for the change.

Maybe it was just this section of the city that was devoid of activity, though all the stage dressing of life remained. Cars were parked, but no one was around to drive them. Houses looked occupied, but no one was in the yards, no one peeked from behind curtains, no drone of televisions mumbled through the walls, no dogs barked from behind fences, and no horns or traffic noise rose from the distance. Only an airplane rising as a dot in the sky with a vapor trail cutting the sky behind it broke the illusion that they were the last two people on Earth.

With matching satchels on their hips, they walked down the middle of the road like they had goods to sell or a religion to peddle, to any soul who dared to show themselves.

The residential gave way to business and commercial property, but there was no break in the apocalyptic emptiness. Some businesses were marked open, while others showed closed.

Hank wondered if he explored one of those places if he'd find half-eaten food still warm on the plates. Maybe potatoes burning black on the flat top grills. Maybe there'd be IBMs as big as old televisions still warming up, green and pixelated, on top of unmanned desks. Perhaps a track printer would still be slowly cranking out last month's sales reports on green and white lined paper.

The landscape became chemical tanks on both sides, and Hank tried to remember if he had mentioned to Savannah how strange and otherworldly this all was. He was having trouble remembering much of anything anymore. He'd thought he was onto the secret behind this. He'd killed a man for his phone and started following down the leads as best he could while bopping through time and across the country. Always the same country? Couldn't remember now. What city had he been in when he first saw Savannah when she lost her satchel? And was that the first time? Rusty Nail seemed to indicate otherwise. They had plotted in the next century a couple days ago. They plotted in this place on a side of town that still had people yesterday. Was it yesterday? Now he couldn't remember any of their plans.

A white monolith of a warehouse rose in the distance, beyond the giant white tanks on the right side of the road, with barren desert stretching out flat and forever across from it. Everything had been so green up to this point.

There could have been loading docks along the long side of the nondescript building. The sun blazed off the unbroken and the untarnished white of the structure until all the details blurred. Maybe this was a distribution center. Maybe it was the end of the world. This had to be the building, though, because there was nothing else beside it, and nothing between it and the flat dead horizon in every other direction.

They were going to go inside, force their way in, but Hank couldn't remember why. What the hell was this place, and why did it matter? This was the "answer," she had said, and he had believed her, but why had he? He couldn't remember.

There was no 138 anywhere on the place, not a single marking that could be construed into a clue.

His fingers found the button on the strap of his satchel. Without looking at the smooth plastic cover, he knew it was red on top, blue on the bottom, and had

138 printed on the band through the middle, same as Savannah's satchel. Same as all porters' satchels, one might assume.

138? It was the rule. It was the room they were drawn to by clues for the next random port. But the rule wasn't perfect. Like there were holes in his memory, there were holes in the rule. Sometimes he ported without it. 138 … 2034 … never 2035. There were missing clues.

The clues were lies. Had she said that, or was it him? It seemed important to remember which one said it before they got there, even though they both walked silently toward the same fate.

The dwarf. He saw him under a pipe in the last row of industrial storage tanks. Andrew? Andy? What had he said to Hank? Was it in New Jersey? Maybe this year, but many ports ago. He couldn't remember that either. His eyes refocused, and the mirage was gone.

He looked forward and saw other figures move along dark patches out in the desert. There was nowhere to hide out there in the open, but there was enough alternating color to fool the eyes or to camouflage what might really be there.

Terry was there, and then he wasn't, a guy he barely remembered who told him something important. Was he older or younger than last time he saw him? Wasn't he dead? He was gone again either way.

A bartender with a scar, she was dead, too, right? But what did dead mean to time travelers? And what did it mean if she was just going to vanish like that?

More figures and dark vehicles materialized near the building. They stood out against the white of the structure. They moved in a frenzy of activity, and then they were gone, along with their nondescript, but always identifiable black SUVs. Did those even exist in this year? He supposed it didn't matter if they weren't really there at all, and he was just seeing things.

Or was it remembering things?

Mr. Train's men or the Clocksmiths working against "the plan?"

"Did you see that?" he asked.

She didn't answer either way.

You aren't missing blocks of time, a voice spoke in his head from somewhere distant. *You switch up chunks out of the middle, and then the pieces shuffle.*

He had no idea when he heard it, or if it was even true.

It's not a Butterfly Effect, another voice added from another time. *It's the reverse. You are one of many stabilizers. Your tiny actions add up to stretching out the timeline and pushing out the ending. Any time you get wise, you get scrambled, blocked, chunked, and tossed back out to monkey through time all over again. All you 138s are trying to solve a puzzle while stabilizing and stretching out the years. We don't avert wars anymore. We push them through time with random human particles, like you, like her, like all the 138s.*

Hank stopped in the middle of the road, "I've done this before."

Savannah stopped, blinked, and looked back at him like she was snapping out of a trance. "What? What are you talking about?"

"I've done this before, Savannah. We have … Maybe we both have. More than once."

She looked toward the building and back at him. "This is it. This is where we need to go for answers."

"I'm not going. Not until I remember more of what I've forgotten. Or figure out what's going on here." He stared at her a moment longer, but then turned around and walked the other way without waiting on her.

She looked back and forth between him and the building. They were so close. She took a while longer to decide what to do next.

Chapter 26

December 16th, 1985 - Salt Lake City, Utah

Hank stole a car. That wasn't something he used to do. He wanted to swear it was only to borrow, and he'd put it back, but he knew it would stay in the parking lot forever. No one would come to claim it. No one would move it back the three blocks, to its rightful place in another parking lot, similar to this one.

He needed something more solid to sit in, to sleep in, to take notes in.

Hank still hadn't found anyone alive, although there were no bloodstains, no burning eggs or meat on stoves, no TVs left on. It was as if the city of Salt Lake had decided they'd had enough, turned everything off, and walked away.

Savannah was gone again. Whether she'd entered the building, or was wandering around the city looking for clues, or she'd decided to join the Salt Lakers and disappear.

There were going to be no more clues for Hank, nothing to find, nowhere else to go, not until he had some answers, no matter how long it took.

Armed with a dozen candy bars, three warm Cokes in bottles and a new legal pad and set of six colored pens, Hank decided to watch, eat, observe, and take note.

But how many times have I made some monumental decision to change what I was doing only to fall right back into the same obsessive patterns all over again? I've been here before.

Was the sky moving quickly, the clouds so fast he couldn't see them? Hank shook his head. It was all an illusion.

All of it? Another shake of his head. Something was happening. He didn't know what. He couldn't put words to it, even when he tried to concentrate, green pen in hand hovering an inch from the blank pages.

He knew he needed to go into the building. It was either the end, or the beginning, of what he was searching for… or it was nothing. Another port. Another jump to another jump to another jump.

Hank felt powerless. He wondered if he always felt this way, or if he was finally dealing with it. Another shake of the head. The red pen hovered. His wrist began to hurt.

Take control of this and stop letting it happen to you.

The car faced the door he thought Savannah was

headed to or had entered.

What if the door opened at five and a stream of workers came out, all wearing futuristic spacesuits? Their shift over, they'd go out for a beer at the closest bar, while the overnight shift, also wearing their spacesuits, came in and went inside. It was just another day of work in the strange building, manipulating fate.

Yet, it wasn't a strange building. It was a normal one, in fact.

Hank had pulled the car into the parking lot next to a dozen other cars. The gate to the area wasn't even closed. There were no guards in the small guard post.

There was a lot of nothing.

Hank opened the windows to let in the heat, his breathing ragged for no reason he could discern. He felt anxious, like he was truly waiting for something to happen.

He scratched his nose with the pen cap stuck on the blunt end of the purple pen.

This wasn't a deja vu moment, although he supposed it could be, and he wouldn't know it. Talking to Savannah about their memories resetting and erasing was an upsetting concept.

He had the windows down but, despite the heat, didn't run the engine and the air conditioning just yet. He felt like he needed to hear something. Anything.

No birds sang in the scant trees, no sound of an airplane overhead, no cars on the highway in the distance. Even the wind was complicit and quiet.

He held the yellow pen ready to write, but what was he supposed to do? He could list off all the things that weren't there.

Who writes in yellow pen anyway?

Hank traded the pen for a candy bar, which was already starting to melt. After finishing it quickly, he licked his fingers and took the top off of an orange pen, but still had nothing to write. His head had been filled with ideas and random thoughts moments ago, but now that he was trying to focus on what needed to be written down, it escaped him. The notebooks in his storage unit amounted to years of gibberish.

Was there a pattern to the years? Hank went through his satchel, sure he'd written down the years and maybe noted a pattern. He knew he would find none even before he started.

He was sweating, but refused to put up the windows.

Something was going to happen. He was sure of it.

He felt sticky. He'd heard (from where he obviously didn't know) it was a dry heat in this part of the country, but he thought it was a lie to make people feel better about living in such an awfully hot place. His clothes clung to him and his feet itched like mad inside his shoes. He wanted to fling his shoes and socks off and out the car window and scratch his feet, but instead he closed his eyes and tried to sleep.

After a few seconds or a few hours, he opened his eyes and wiped the sweat off of his face. He drank one of the very warm Cokes, gagging on the heat from the soda.

If nothing happened by nightfall, he'd drive back to the store and find something to eat for dinner along with something cool to wash it down.

He wasn't going to play this game anymore. He'd sit in this car until he died from heatstroke, or his mind was reset, and he wondered what he was doing.

If he refused to do what *they*, whoever *they* were, wanted him to do, would they take action? Reprogram him remotely to drive away, or go into the building, or stay and do nothing forever? Send the Clocksmith with unmatching eyes to make good on his threats?

"Dig two graves," Hank growled over his dry throat.

And then he heard a noise, so small under normal circumstances he wouldn't have even noticed it, just another sound carried on the wind along with the rest of the small sounds, a minor cacophony.

A door had been opened.

It was Savannah. She stood in the doorway, one hand keeping the door open, the other hand beckoning Hank to join her.

He shook his head.

She looked angry and went back inside.

He could have imagined that, too.

Hank closed his eyes and settled back in the seat.

The touch startled him.

Hank opened his eyes, sweat dripping from his

forehead.

"Time to go and port," Savannah, standing at his window, said. "I think I found a clue. A real one, not where they want us to go."

Hank stared at her.

"Have you ever been to Mesquite, Nevada?" Savannah asked.

Hank didn't really know if he had or not. He got out of the car, grabbed his satchel, and followed her, still not yet in control of his own destiny, despite all his dreams and plans.

Chapter 27

December 17th, 2003 - Mesquite, Nevada

"Rusty Nail, Nevada doesn't exist in 2003," Hank said. "Isn't that weird?"

"I knew that," Savannah said. "It's not weird. It's just a fact. Vegas didn't exist until the mob built it. Same way when they built Rusty Nail in twenty-twenty … something."

They stood in the relative chill of the converted storage container outside the one story house on a sandy lot. Savannah held onto the open sliding door. The fluorescents glowed an odd, dull light. Fans spun somewhere, but didn't move much air.

The computer that sprawled across the folding table by the wall was not any particular model, but was constructed from a mish mash of parts that were old, even for 2003. It had taken two hours to warm up, and no one had come here during that entire time.

A radio was set on low in the corner to a talk station. It came on at the same time they flipped on the power for the computer. At the moment, they were in a commercial break. An ad for the movie *Pay Check* with Ben Affleck gave way to an ad for the new release of *Return of the King*.

Hank closed the atlas and put it back on the bookshelf with all the Dean Koontz, Brian C. Redd, and Randy Wayne White novels. Mixed in with those were a scattering of conspiracy theory and unexplained phenomenon books. Hank flipped through the copies of *The Desert Valley Times* newspapers on top of the shelf.

"It's just weird," he said.

"Why's it weird, Hank, if that is even your real name?"

He laughed and looked up at her. She stared out across the Mojave Desert all around them. They had passed plenty of people in town between the casinos, but this empty spot could have been just like the strange section of Salt Lake City. This container sat almost on the Arizona state line. It was an 80 mile drive for them up from Vegas, along Interstate 15, where they had ported from the strange building to room 138 in some casino hotel out there in Vegas. The mountain in the distance was called the Virgin Mountain, and they had passed a sign for the Virgin River.

The car Savannah had stolen from the Vegas casino

lot was now parked by the small house beside this container. The windows were down and they'd left the radio on. It competed with the radio beside the computer.

The stolen car was some foreign model with foreign plates called a Chery A11. Hank had never heard of it. It seemed a conspicuous choice of getaway vehicle. There was no arguing with her. You just went along or got left behind. Some singer cried from the car's radio, "Hey Ya!" over and over.

"It's weird," Hank said, "because Rusty Nail is a weird name for a town built in the twenty-first century."

Savannah shrugged. "I guess."

"Where's our big clue?" Hank flipped through the newspapers. "The real clue you dragged me back into that building for."

"It's coming, I'm sure … What do you mean, back into the building?"

"We've been there a bunch of times before."

"You remember?"

The bombastic talk radio host returned from the commercial break in full rant. He declared that finding Saddam Hussein in his spider hole was a game changer. They'd find the WMD's now, and Bush had reelection locked up. None of the references sounded familiar to Hank.

"I don't remember going in exactly, but I remember my mind … our minds being wiped over and over every time we tried."

Savannah shook her head. "Did your mind get wiped this time?"

"I don't think so."

"Then, you must be remembering wrong because it didn't happen, did it?"

"It happened."

She snorted and folded her arms, staring across the desert.

"Maybe there's a real big clue in here," Hank said. He rifled the papers. "Tiger Woods won the President's Cup … no, he shared the cup. So, that was nice of him, I guess."

"Calm down, Hank."

"Terror attacks in Moscow and Saudi Arabia and Israel … 'tis the season, I guess." Hank dumped a couple of the papers into the floor.

"Chill out, asshole. Don't make me sorry I brought you."

"Oh, yeah, thanks for that. You're a real peach of a travel companion, when we're not getting shot at, or you're not leaving me to die. I've been shot in the same shoulder twice that I remember. It's started hurting when it gets cold."

The talk station had switched to a condemnation of the activist Massachusetts Supreme Court lifting the ban on same sex marriage. The radio in the A11 declared that her milkshake brings all the boys to the yard.

"Fuck you," Savannah said.

"Howard Dean may run for president next year. We should send him a spoiler alert." Hank dropped another paper. "According to these ads the Mesquite Star and the Peppermill both have free buffets for slot players. We should —"

She clenched her fists and stepped inside. "Just shut up, you fucking child. I'm trying to solve this, and you're throwing a temper tantrum over what you think you don't remember."

"You two again," a man holding two armloads of plastic bags bulging with groceries said from between the container entrance and the stolen car. "Get away from my computer before you erase something important."

Hank dropped all the papers on the floor. "You know us? We've been here before?"

The man had a scraggly grey and black beard. He wore a pink tank top and cutoff jean shorts with white strings hanging down into his thick leg hair. "Jesus, you've come here, to my last two places, to my next place, in Rusty Nail ... You've been here, you've been now, you will have been a pain in my ass forever and ever. Amen."

"At the facility in Salt Lake," Savannah said, "we found —"

"Salt Lake! Of course. Was is it normal-timeline Salt Lake or the trippy-between-dimensions version of the Salt Lake building? You know? Don't bother answering because it doesn't matter. You find the same thing every time, don't you? Nothing, Savannah Whatever-Last-

Name-You're-Using-Now, you found nothing. You found nothing all the other times, you'll find nothing the next time, and it always either leads you back to me or it resets you, and I have to explain everything all over to you again, like you two are my favorite time travel dementia-stricken aunt and uncle."

"Who are you?" Hank asked.

"Brian Castro Redd. Same as every other time." He lifted the grocery bags in both hands. "Suppose I should feed you before I kick your asses back out to the four winds again, huh?"

Hank waved a hand at the papers scattered on the floor. "The Mesquite Star and Peppermill are having a buffet deal."

Brian Redd moved toward the house. "Peppermill becomes the Oasis and both places close when the Recession hits in the late 2000's."

"You jump through time like us?" Savannah asked.

Brian kicked open the side door to his house with his hands full. He turned in the doorway. "Not like you. I figured out how to do all my porting in my own house. Then, I figured out how to make it stop for me. I just have to be sure not to run into my younger time-jumping self." He closed his eyes, but then opened them and looked at the sky. His eyes darted back and forth as his lips moved. Then, he nodded. "Today is Wednesday. A younger version of me is going to appear here next Tuesday. I have to be scarce then. I guess all the time traveling versions of me have to be younger now, right? Since I'm aging again ... Get out of my office and get in here so we can get this pointless conversation over with. And if that damn car is stolen, at least pull it around back so the plates don't show. It's a wonder you idiots aren't dead already."

"Wait," Hank called.

Brian turned around, still holding his groceries. "What, Hank Smith?"

"Why did you add your middle initial on your books after the sixties?"

"Interesting. Something new. You've never asked me that before. This could be an interesting visit after all." Brian C. Redd smiled. "Back in the sixties, when I stopped porting and starting writing to really leave my mark on the world, having the middle name Castro didn't exactly make the books fly off the shelf."

He disappeared inside the house, but left the door open.

Hank and Savannah looked at each other. Then, they followed Brian.

Chapter 28

December 17th, 2003 - Mesquite, Nevada

Brian C. Redd winked at Savannah. "I'd ask you if you want me to make pancakes or burgers, but I already know the answer."

"Which is…" Savannah said.

"Always pancakes."

"Then, I want a burger," Hank said, thinking he'd change it up.

Brian winked at Hank. "You always ask for a burger."

"Then switch them," Savannah said.

Brian shrugged. "We've done this a hundred different ways. None of that minutiae matters. It's as simple as it seems: you want pancakes or burgers for dinner?"

"You got out of the loop. Was it as simple as not

looking for clues?" Hank asked.

Brian stared at him so long, Hank grew uncomfortable and looked away.

"I want to show you something. You've seen it before, and I'll explain it the same way to see if you react the same." Brian went into another room, leaving Savannah and Hank in the small kitchen.

"You think this guy's nuts?" Savannah asked.

Hank shrugged. "I like his books." He almost said it like an apology.

"How do you like him as a retired time traveler that knows more about us than we do?" she asked.

"The time traveler who's making us pancakes and burgers for dinner? Who we've met countless times, but don't remember… because we're also time travelers? I think nuts is pretty damn relative right now." Hank stood. "What if I made burgers?"

"I don't think it would matter, or you've done it a hundred times already."

Hank shook his head. "I doubt we've been here that much. He's aging again, and stuck in this time, which means we would have to be showing up every few days in order for it to be that much. I think."

"Shut up. You're giving me a headache." Savannah closed her eyes.

"He said a younger version was coming to visit, and he knew the day." Hank looked for burgers in the refrigerator and freezer but didn't find any. "What if he's constantly bombarded with other versions of himself coming to visit?"

Savannah shook her head. "I think only one version ported, and now he's stopped. He lives here and has to dodge another version of himself. Wait. How many versions would be here? Only one. Right?"

"Maybe." Hank went through the bags of groceries Brian had brought in but found no burgers. A lot of potato chip and pretzel bags as well as a twelve-pack of beer. "This guy loves his chips and beer."

Hank heard Brian coming back down the hallway and stood at the sink.

"I found it," Brian said and handed a sheet of paper to Hank.

"What is it?"

"You tell me. What do you see?"

The question rung in his head. It rang like he'd heard it a hundred times before.

Hank stared at the paper, which had an odd drawing on it. Weird, swirling colors and a kaleidoscope of smaller images. It was something he'd seen before. He knew it.

"Tell me what you see, Hank." Brian stared intently. "First impression."

Hank had a few ideas running through his head, like he'd stored them from previous encounters. He knew they'd done this dance many times. Instead of answering, he handed the sheet back to Brian. "How many times have we been here?"

Brian frowned. "Dozens. I lost count. I know my

future visits, but your future visits will be a surprise for me. What do you see in the picture?"

Hank glanced at Savannah, who still had her eyes shut.

"Do you remember the time you made us tacos?" Hank asked.

"I remember all of the food I've made for you two."

Hank shook his head. "You never made us tacos. You never made us pancakes or burgers, either. This isn't real. None of this is what it looks like."

Brian tried to give Hank the picture, but Hank stepped back.

Savannah had her eyes open and was standing.

"This is a setup, Savannah. Another ruse to get us to go the wrong way. I see it now," Hank said. "How long have you been trapped in 2003?"

"I'm living it in real time. I'm a civilian since the 60s, Mr. Smith," Brian said quickly. He still had the paper in hand.

Hank took it from Brian's hand, but crumpled it up and tossed it in the sink.

"You're making a big mistake," Brian said. He licked his lips. "If you tell me what you see in the picture, all will be revealed. Then, you'll have a choice. I know which one you'll make, but you have a choice. This could be the end of the road for you. Both of you."

"What do you mean?" Savannah asked.

"It's true. If Hank tells me what he sees, what he really sees, in the picture, it's your chance to get off this rollercoaster ride and be done. You can stop this madness. Live wherever you want, whenever you want. Just like me." Brian winked. "But you won't. You'll remember enough and know you have something to finish. I don't know all of it, but I know you are in more control than you think you are. Not remembering it all at once is part of it, for some reason."

"What does that all mean?" Savannah asked.

Brian shrugged. "I retired. You working stiffs keep coming to visit."

"Except… we don't. Which means…" Hank looked at Savannah. "He's lying. None of this is real."

Brian reached for Hank, but Hank slapped Brian's hands away and drew back.

"Oh, crap, this is that day," Brian said. He ran for the door.

Hank lashed out and clipped Brian across the side of the jaw. Brian reeled, and Hank tripped him to the linoleum floor.

Before Savannah or Hank could pounce, Brian was up and skidding across the floor, heading toward the exit.

Hank dove and missed Brian, who ran out the front door and kept going. "You're an asshole, Hank. A paranoid asshole!"

"Should we try to stop him?" Savannah asked, helping Hank off the floor.

"No. He's not important. I think he was here to block us. He was going to reset us. I think he needed me to say something specific so something else could happen. I know it makes no sense. You don't have to say it. I just have a feeling… I'm on to something big."

Savannah picked up the balled paper from the sink. "What is it?"

Hank didn't know and didn't want to know. He took it from her and ripped it into small pieces, throwing them in the garbage can.

"How could you possibly know this wasn't real? I don't remember tacos either way," Savannah said.

Hank sighed. "Neither did I. It was a bluff. I just knew he wanted me to answer him badly, because…" Hank snapped his fingers. "It was a keyword. We've been brainwashed."

"Brainwashed? By Mr. Train or your favorite pulp writer?"

Hank shook his head. "That's not exactly right, but it's closer than I've ever been to the truth. The clues might not mean anything to other people. They might not even be real. But we see them. They're keywords that get us to move. To respond. A certain word gets a reaction. He was trying to wipe us out or kill us or… I don't know. Maybe he's really a Clocksmith and didn't expect us to show up at his house when we deviated from the track."

"If we've been here before," Savannah said, "then this is the track, the same one chugging around in circles."

Hank shook his head. "It wasn't going to end well

for us. Maybe he was only there to reset us to start over. I'm really close to figuring this out."

"Which means we need to be really careful, because if we get too close, they will reset us. We probably shouldn't be waiting around here if he's connected to someone against us." Savannah sighed. "Where are we going?"

"Time to set our own rules. We head back into Las Vegas and find a room 138 to sleep."

"Follow the clues?"

Hank shook his head. "No. We ignore all clues. If something seems leading to your brain, it means it is. From now on, we move randomly."

"But what if we're stuck here, in this time, then?"

Hank smiled. "We won't be. Trust me. Brian C. Redd was lying. He's not trapped here. I think he tried it and failed. I think he's porting in and out and was sent to intercept us because we're getting too close to the truth."

She didn't look convinced. "At least you didn't kill anyone this time … What's the damn truth?"

Hank wished he had a real answer.

Chapter 29

December 20th, 1983 - Denver, Colorado

Hank slapped the side of the radiator in the hotel room. He pulled his hand back as it burned him. He cussed and stepped away, clutching his wrist. The metal was hot as hell, but it wasn't heating the room past a few feet. Apparently 1983 was a bad year for keeping warm.

There had been a blizzard over Thanksgiving that had paralyzed the city. They were still digging themselves out when Savannah and Hank showed up. They wanted to travel to another random city, according to their newest master plan, but the roads weren't cooperating. Did the puppet masters have control of the weather, too?

Hank flexed his swollen hand and suddenly had the urge to cry. It wasn't the pain. Maybe it was frustration. Maybe it was the feeling of being lost.

The room, the same 138 they'd ported into a couple

days ago, had a TV that wasn't picking up any channels. A boxy radio played low in the background, and he heard it now that he was finally sitting still. It was a sports channel, or they were doing a sports report.

Broadcaster One had a Brooklyn accent. "Yogi Berra is skipper for the Yankees for the second time. I guess he didn't do a bad enough job the first time, huh? What do you think?"

Broadcaster Two jumped in with a little bit of a twang, "I think it may be more of a case of every other option doing a worse job. Fifth and Sixth place finishes aren't exactly a great start to the decade. If it got much worse, they might have brought Yogi back as a catcher instead of a manager."

They laughed. Broadcaster One added, "As Yogi might say about his second turn as manager, third time's the charm."

Hank's eyes and mind drifted. The art on the wall above the king bed was an abstract swirl in kaleidoscope colors. *Tell me what you see, Hank.* He looked away. A brochure on the side table advertised bars around town. The Salty Sailor … The Rusty Nail … Redd's Place …

Would these be the clues, if I was looking for them, Hank wondered. *Back to Salt Lake City? Or a future town in Nevada? Or back to Redd's house for round 2?*

He flipped the brochure over. The back was an ad for a train museum.

Broadcaster One was said, "Steve Howe of the L.A. Dodgers got a one year vacation from Major League

Baseball. That's a long suspension, but not the lifetime ban some were calling for. Probably a bunch of Reds fans, I'm guessing."

Broadcaster Two laughed. "He'll have more time to powder his nose."

"Come on, Marty. We don't do that kind of show."

"Why you making this weird, Tim?"

Hank spun the tuning dial through the gulf of static between stations. A wavering signal had a more professional sounding newswoman reciting, "The last 80 United States combat soldiers in Grenada were brought home as the …"

He rolled the dial again. He thought he heard the opening synthesizer for the song "Sweet Dreams." He couldn't remember who sang that one, but he turned off the radio and headed for the door before he found out.

Walking past the elevator on the first floor, he migrated from the cold hallway into the dank restaurant area. Savannah already had a booth. A pair of businessmen a few tables over were the only other patrons in the hotel restaurant. The colors in the restaurant looked left over from the 1970s. There was a spiral in the pastel blocks in the stained carpet. Hank kept his eyes up and away from the pattern as he sat down.

He didn't bother looking at the menu. Everything tasted like cardboard. He would probably order the cardboard flavored chicken-fried steak with cold-in-the-middle microwaved white gravy.

There was a pepper shaker on the table, but not salt. There was plenty of salt to steal off of other vacant tables, but he didn't bother, yet.

"You want to make a break for it?" Savannah asked. "We'll make snowshoes out of the meatloaf and hike down to Mexico."

Hank held his stomach, wishing she hadn't brought up the meatloaf. "Let me eat one more meal here, and then I should be ready to freeze to death."

"Ninth return mission," Businessman One said a little too loud. He wore the brownest suit Hank could imagine. He also had the thickest mustache a human lip could support.

Businessman Two wore a suit that was a few shades away from skin-tone tan. It bothered Hank down where the meatloaf still settled in his gut. The guy's tie was grey. Hank decided what bothered him was the suit should be the color of the tie. "That can't be right."

"It is, man. It really is. We'll have bases on the Moon and be on our way to Mars by the turn of the century."

"I doubt it."

Businessman One waved a hand at his partner before shoveling a spoonful of corn, flavored like gravel as Hank recalled, into his gob. He spoke over the kernels. "Space exploration is expanding exponentially."

"They just did another nuke test over in Nevada. We'll be wasted by the Commies before we get to Mars."

"All the more reason to explore other planets."

"I'm going to skip the flying car and keep my wheels on the ground, thanks."

Businessman One pointed toward the front door as he wiped his mouth, still chewing corn. "On a day like today, sky cars would be great … What do you think, Bud?"

It took Hank a second to realize the guy with gravy and corn in his mustache was talking to him. "Oh, ugh, Shuttle Program will peter out at some point in the twenty-first."

As the guy wiped his mustache, he asked, "The twenty-first of what?"

Hank squinted. "The twenty-first century."

"Get out of here."

"What about flying cars, Mr. Spock?" Businessman Two in his skin-colored suit asked.

"We'll get the tricorders with all the knowledge in the world, but no flying cars," Hank said.

"We got encyclopedias and libraries for that stuff. We need to travel to the stars," Businessman One took on another bite of corn gravel.

"What would you even do with all that knowledge hanging from your utility belt?" Businessman Two asked.

"Mostly look up porn," Hank said.

"What the hell?"

A woman in a hotel uniform walked up to interrupt Hank's prophecies. Hank said, "Country-fried steak with whatever canned veggies are warmest."

The woman stared a moment. "No, sir, sorry. I'm from the front desk. A package was delivered for you."

"For him?" Savannah asked. "I don't think so."

"Both of you." The woman held up a package wrapped neatly in Santa Claus paper. "You're 138, aren't you?"

"Boy, are we," Hank said.

"Enjoy your stay." She placed the gift on the edge of the table before walking away.

"Delivery?!" Hank called after her, "Through the mail?"

She didn't pause as she walked away. "Hand delivered, I believe."

"What did the guy look like?" Savannah called.

"It was last shift. I don't know. Sorry. Enjoy your stay." She was in the lobby by the time she finished talking.

They both just stared at it.

The businessmen had moved on from their dreams of the stars to the topic of television. They discussed "the *Thriller* short film by Jackson Five" being Satanic, as the front desk clerk talked about the package. After she left, the men moved on to rumors that Henry Kissinger and Gerald and Betty Ford were going to be guest stars on Dynasty tomorrow night.

"What is this?" Savannah finally whispered.

"It's Christmas," Hank said.

He lifted the white cardboard tag taped to Santa Claus's round belly. It read: FOR THE SMITHS —

SAFE TRAVELS. Hank showed it to Savannah, and she shook her head.

As Hank ripped off the paper, it bothered him how thin the wrapping felt. He let it fall to the floor under the table as he and Savannah stared at the cover of the book. "Last Bar on the Left After the End of the World by Brian C. Redd."

Hank opened it while his heart thudded in his chest. It was a prepublication review copy. The copyright was 2035.

An unsigned penned note read: *I think we got off on the wrong foot this last time. We never fought in any of your other visits, so that was new. You misinterpreted the situation. Don't play into their traps. Mr. Train is starting to pay attention to the two of you and that's the last thing you want. Stop back by my place and we'll try again. I'm there all the time in every timeline from 1979 forward.*

He checked the bio. It said Brian C. Redd split his time between Mesquite and Rusty Nail.

Hank closed the book. "How? Why?"

"Do you believe any of it?"

Hank shook his head. "I don't know … no. Maybe we're drawing attention. That much seems true."

Savannah shook her head. "Maybe it doesn't matter, but I want to beat these people. I want to get ahead and be free of this."

"So, meatloaf snowshoes?"

She smiled and turned the book over so the cover art of a snowy street scene no longer showed. "If they can find us here, then they'll find us if we try to freeze in the snow. Let's port somewhere warm and keep going."

Hank took a deep breath and nodded. After a moment, he picked up the book and started reading the really advance copy as he waited for a waitress.

Chapter 30

December 23, 2019 - Jacksonville, Florida

Despite being close to Christmas, it felt anything but to Hank. The bright blue cloudless sky, eighty degrees, and slight breeze off the river felt like it was April in any other city north of here.

They were seated in Hemming Park, a few blocks from the river itself. Hank didn't need to see it to know it was close; the smell drifted around him, the smell of the homeless as well.

"Can we go somewhere else?" Savannah frowned as two homeless men wandered past, eyeing her. "This is depressing."

"It's warm, and I don't see any snow," Hank said. "I think I was born in the Southeast or Southwest. I'm sure I grew up in beautiful weather."

"Or you were born in Maine or Illinois and swore

you'd never stay," Savannah said.

Hank shrugged. "Let's go find a cup of coffee."

They walked down the block, past the library, stopping outside a bookstore that also had a cafe to the left.

"A book and a coffee? Sounds like heaven," Savannah said.

They entered Chamblin's, and Hank took in a new, great smell: coffee mingling with old books.

"I'll get us two coffees and maybe a snack," Savannah said, leaving Hank to wander the packed rows of books. He was sure he was well-read, even before he'd begun porting. Often, he'd find a book he wanted to read, and realize a few pages into it he'd already read it.

History books were fun to read, especially since he'd lived through so much of it. The Cuban missile crisis? He remembered it like it was yesterday.

The world ended in October of 1962. We've been walking around dead ever since and don't know it.

He couldn't remember where he read that, but it seemed important.

Who knew where all and when all he had been? Maybe he'd been at several battles during the Civil War, the great fire in San Francisco, and the Gold Rush. He'd definitely watched the Moon landing and the ill-fated teacher in the space shuttle explosion. Hank wondered what the two businessmen from 1983 thought about the future of space exploration after that. He could read about a President he'd watch on and off over time, depending on his ports.

He ran his fingers over the spines of the histories. He paused on one for a long moment and then moved on.

There was one book on the Spanish flu from the early 20th century. That made him uneasy. The end of 2019 was a dicey time. By February of 2020, the pandemic had started and things were full-blown by March. Cases had started in Asia by late 2019 and scientists in the late 2020s and early 2030s believed the spread had started earlier, when no one knew what they were looking for. If they hadn't ported by January, they'd need to take precautions. By 2021, the variants and mutations would begin to spread.

He checked the Brian C. Redd books out of habit. Every title seemed familiar. One was new to him. *The Clockmaker's Men*. He'd missed this one, or forgot reading it. It was published in 1984. The 80's were a real hit and miss decade for Redd's work.

Hank considered the title for a long moment, but then left it. Once you found a reason to punch a writer in the face, it changed the way you looked at their work. He finally left without the title in his hand.

He joined Savannah at an outside table and sipped his coffee, which was hot, strong, and delicious. "I'm sure I was always a big coffee drinker, too."

"Where is all this coming from?"

Hank didn't really know. It was merely a guess.

"What books did you look at?" Savannah asked.

"History books." He left out the fact that he'd checked out Redd's work again, despite everything that had happened.

She stared at Hank and nodded slowly. "Like what? Tell me the first book that comes to mind."

"The 1906 San Francisco earthquake," Hank said, as he recalled a long pause on that spine.

Savannah pointed at the car parked at the curb. "California plates. An 'I Survived Alcatrazz bumper sticker.' "

Hank smiled. "You can't stop finding clues."

"Old habit," Savannah said. "Besides, I'm sick of fighting it. Where has it gotten us? Nowhere." She took a sip of coffee. "Maybe we're not meant to veer off just yet. If we're still finding clues, it means we're still on course."

Hank shook his head. "On course for what? To keep slipping into the endless loop? I don't think so." He picked up his coffee. "I thought you were going to get us a snack."

Savannah grinned. "It was mostly vegan food. I didn't know if you like that sort of thing, especially in your past life you seem to know so much about."

Hank returned her grin. She was making fun of him. "I have no idea if I like it or don't." He pushed his chair out. "I'll get us something."

"No." Savannah put up a hand. "I know just the thing. Be right back."

Hank stared at the people going by, those in business suits and the homeless on the corner watching for an easy mark.

He Waited for someone to step out of the crowd with a new clue, a new threat, or a new problem for them.

Savannah came back outside, lingering in the open door. "You hear what's playing? Journey. You know where they're from?"

Hank groaned. "Don't say San Francisco."

"I don't have to say it. You already know the answer." Savannah put down a croissant and a bagel on the table. "Your choice which one you want. I could go either way."

"I was hoping for something sweet," Hank said.

"You mean like… these?" She pulled two chocolate chip cookies from the bag.

"Exactly."

They ate in silence for a few minutes, sipping the last of their coffee and finishing the food while watching the people come and go.

"You going to buy a book?" Savannah asked.

"Maybe. It seems like the thing to do before we are on our way."

"Off to where?"

"There's really only one thing to do, clues or no clues," Hank said.

Savannah frowned. "I don't like where this is going."

"You mean where *we're* going… back to Mesquite to see Brian C. Redd, and figure out, once and for all, what his role in all this is."

"I don't want to go back there," Savannah said. She put a hand on Hank's shoulder. "We need to go to San Francisco. It's what the signs say."

Hank casually pushed her hand away. "I thought you were the one who told me not to rely on the clues. Didn't you say it was leading us in the wrong direction? Maybe even in an endless circle?" He shook his head. "We go to Nevada and figure this out."

"I'm not going," Savannah said. "I'm headed to San Fran."

"Then, you're going on your own."

Savannah looked like she was going to cry. "Please… please, come with me."

Hank knew she wasn't telling him something. But what?

Savannah looked away. "I've had bad dreams about you. Really bad. I don't want to talk about it, but…" She turned back to Hank. "Your last stop is in Nevada, and Brian Redd is the one who ends it for you. I don't want to lose you."

Chapter 31

December 26th, 1996 - Mesquite, Nevada

Brian Redd's kitchen looked exactly the same as the last time they had been here, seven years in the future. They didn't bother with his writing trailer. He just opened his front door for them when they knocked and let them in. They sat at the table with his mail piled up on the corner of the formica surface.

As he cooked, Brian played the same song on repeat by an indie rock band called The Fucking Champs over and over. Brian reached out to turn it up and knocked over a tiny fern growing out of a tiny overturned plastic 49ers helmet. Brian cursed as he retrieved the plant from the sink, and Hank was thankful Brian forgot to turn the song up.

"It just came out … this album … in the natural timeline," Brian said. "When I escaped the loops and settled here permanently, back in the sixties, to live out my life in a straight line, I brought back my favorite albums as CDs, tapes, digital files, and such … and the players I needed for them, of course. Had to keep it all hidden until the CD player was actually invented. I was worried the thing was going to bust, and I'd be stuck with tiny round mirrors I couldn't listen to anymore."

"Why are you listening to this one song over and over again, then?" Savannah asked.

He covered one of the pans, turned down the heat, and pointed at her with a spatula. "I lost it. This CD. Over ten years ago, I lost it. The old me, the version of me that was still porting, set this place up back at the end of the 70s, and I kept coming here whenever I needed to. I had a couple places before this in the 50s and 60s. I'll have another later in the future. All of us have something similar. Right? I have a notebook that lists every time I came here during a port. When a visit from the old me comes up, I bail until the old time traveling me leaves. Fortunately, I have a few months before I have to get scarce again. I think he took my old copy of the CD one time when I left it out, but I don't remember doing that back when I was him. I started keeping track of when you guys show up, too. I'm not used to you remembering me, though. That's new."

"Do you remember me hitting you?" Hank asked.

Brian stared at him like maybe Hank might be kidding. He took another pan off the burner and started chopping something on a plastic cutting board. "Was that in the past or the future?"

"A few years from now," Hank said. "Same house. Same you."

Brian said, "That would be new, too. I hope I remember to duck now that you warned me. That's going to suck. Every time I see you now, I'm going to think, oh, crap, is today the day Hank decides to punch me?! No, I'm traveling through time at the normal pace of normal people now. I write my books and keep myself locked into history so that they can't afford to erase me. If I still have books coming out in the future, it would change too much to rub me out before my catalog's complete. Time travel protection … literary style. You know what I mean?"

"Who is they?" Savannah asked. "Who could track down and kill you or us?"

Brian swept the cut pieces off of the chopping board into the last pan left on the stove and covered it again. "What do you remember?"

"Never mind what we remember," Hank said. "Tell us everything that's behind this. No more secrets, lies, or double talk."

Brian laughed. "Blow this case wide open, huh? See, I'm really careful not to write this scene into a novel. The scene where everything is spelled out in an information dump by a magical character with all the answers."

Hank and Savannah just stared at him.

Brian walked around the table. "Okay, I have something to show you that will clear everything up."

Hank grabbed Brian by the wrist and halted him. Hank stood up. "If you go to get that spiral again, I'm going to punch you harder than I did seven years from now."

Brian stared at Hank a moment, and then smiled. "Is that why you hit me before? I mean, later? That is new, too. Okay, no resets. I'm as curious as you to see how this plays out."

Hank pushed Brian back against the wall and held him by his collar. "Why are you resetting us each time we come here?"

"I don't," Brian said. "Salt Lake does. I try to unscramble your brain so that you don't lose everything. Sometimes it works, and sometimes it doesn't. I'm glad to see that you remember this much."

"Tell me who is doing this." Hank said.

"The food is going to dry out and then burn," Brian said. "Do you mind?"

Hank let him go, but watched him closely. Brian plated each of them Rice-A-Roni with hotdogs cut up in it.

"Really?" Savannah asked.

Brian poured himself a cup of purple Kool Aid and started eating. Hank sat back down as Brian was talking.

"It's good." Brian waved at the plates as he separated the catalogs from the envelopes in his pile of mail and threw the catalogs away with a crash in the bottom of the plastic trash can with no liner. "I need to go shopping again. I have bay scallops and abalone in the freezer, but they're freezer burned. It's hard to plan when you're stuck in that weird time between Christmas and New Year's. It's like you're suspended outside of time. You're not really moving forward, and you haven't really left the past year behind yet either. The rules of normal time just don't apply when you're in that in-between place like this."

"Who do we need to see to stop this?" Hank asked.

"It depends on what you mean by stopping this, Hank." Brian chewed up and swallowed a chunk of hotdog. He tossed an appeal letter from some charity into the trash unopened. "Do you mean free yourself and live slow-forward like I've done, or do you mean break the chains, behead our captors, and overthrow the empire?"

Hank stared for a long moment. "Who is doing this to us?"

Brian nodded, shoveled in another bite, and frowned as he opened a utility bill, before he said, "Mr. Train. It's always Mr. Train. He controls everything. He throws the switches, and he disconnects and reconnects the tracks as he sees fit to keep the trains running on time. But most of all, he tries to keep the trains from crashing in 2012, 2020, 2029, 2034, 2035, 2036 … and so on. One encounter at a hotel in 1958 loosens a thread drawn too tight in the future. One life sent on a different course in 1984 matters just the right way in a few decades. A couple reconnects instead of breaking up or vice versa. One course of events reversed in one small town of seemingly no consequence keeps the world from derailing. Mr. Train doesn't believe in the Butterfly Effect. He believes in simply finding the right track at the right moment to keep the trains running in steady, endless loops long enough for him to add some extra track. Nothing ever big or noteworthy enough to require a change in a history book to go on someone's shelf or on their coffee table. Never flipping Texas blue and changing the president, or to paint San Francisco red and erase the hippies before Woodstock. Nothing like that, but it changes something. Something only he thinks he can see. He thinks if he runs the right train back and forth through history, fires the wrong conductor, recruits the right porter to dip back and forth through time, with just enough memory to keep them running from one room 138 to another on his schedule, that maybe, just maybe, he can push the end of the world back to 2037 and then 2038. He won't end a pandemic, but he might keep it from destroying the whole world. I'm not sure what year and date he's gotten out to, at this point. I quit a long time ago. What's the furthest out you two remember going in time in this loop you're on now?"

They didn't answer, and he shrugged. There was a long pause as they watched Brian eat and read what looked like a hand-written fan letter.

Savannah asked, "Have you ever met him?"

"I've seen him, I think. I was still mostly in the dark like you two when I quit," Brian said, "but to meet someone means that you know him. No one knows

Mr. Train. No one can. Although, I'm just 1996 Brian. Future Brian you punched in the face may have figured out things I haven't yet. You should go apologize to him and see what he knows."

"Back to Mr. Train … He's keeping the world from ending?" Hank asked. "How? How does it end?"

"He tinkers in the past, like I told you." Brian pushed away his greasy plate and tossed the fan letter. Apparently, he read them, but did not answer them. "I don't remember how it all ends, if I ever knew. Some future version of me has sent things back. I've sent myself messages telling me what I need to do, what I need to avoid, or how to stay out of trouble with the Clocksmiths and with Mr. Train. But I've never told myself how it ends. Maybe I never find out. Unlike you, I'm getting older, so I can't live forever anymore … Are you going to eat that?"

He took Savannah's plate and started eating again.

"How do you know it is you sending the messages, and not Mr. Train or someone else still using you?" Savannah asked.

He tapped his forehead with the prongs of his fork. "I have a secret code only I know."

"What if someone tortured you in the future to take your code, or what if you go senile and just tell someone?" she asked.

He paused in chewing, but then shrugged and kept eating. "Hadn't thought of that."

"How is future you sending messages back in

time?" Hank asked.

"Don't know yet, but obviously I'll find out. Future me gets so smart."

"Where do we find Mr. Train, and what do we need to do when we find him?" Hank asked.

"He is everywhere and nowhere. Figuring out where he is at any one time in history is just …" Brian tossed an envelope full of coupons, and he froze on the last letter, as he stared at it. "Hold on."

He opened it, tore up the envelope into small pieces, and only then unfolded the single sheet of white paper. After he stared, he shook his head.

"Brian?" Savannah said.

"Well," Brian said, "That's new."

He turned the sheet around for them to see. HeLp ThEm GeT 2 sAn fRaNcIsCo. i FiGuReD oUt HoW 2 EnD tHiS. bUt i NeEd hAnK & sAvAnNaH.

"Your super secret code is alternating capitals and lowercase?" Hank asked.

Brian wadded up the page. "There's stuff on the envelope, too."

"San Francisco," Savannah said as she turned her eyes on Hank.

"I don't trust him in this time or any time," Hank said. "How can we trust some future version of him?"

Brian C. Redd returned to eating.

Chapter 32

December 30th, 2034 - San Francisco, California

They'd arrived in San Francisco to see a city already bustling with activity for New Year's Eve, and the party that would begin… until the clock struck midnight and the world ended.

"We still don't know how this ends," Hank said. "Will it be here one second and gone the next? Are we looking at Pacific Time or Eastern Time? Will Australia go dark first?"

Savannah didn't answer. They were walking down the sidewalk, having left their hotel and new room 138, to seek out some lunch.

"I was here a few times," Savannah said. "Once there was an earthquake. Another time the baseball team won the World Series. I saw the Golden Gate Bridge being built."

"How do you suddenly remember all of those times?" Hank asked.

Savannah frowned and looked away. "I don't know. I was trying to make conversation. That's all."

Hank felt like she was lying. The last few days, after leaving the company of Brian Redd, she'd been quiet. Going through the motions. Not even bothering to look for the clues since she was sure, after the note, they needed to head to San Francisco.

Hank was starting to feel like the only guy out of the loop.

Dropping in two days before the end of the world wasn't a coincidence to Hank, despite what she said.

"What if we're trapped here for the next couple of days? Will we die or just reset? Should we be finding clues so we can leave tonight? I feel like I've been this close to the edge before, and I don't like it." Hank stopped when Savannah did, in front of a deli.

"You want a sandwich?"

"No. I want answers." Hank was losing his patience with her. With all of this.

"Well…" Savannah stared at Hank. There was a battle going on in her head. Hank could sense it. "I'm going inside and getting a hot pastrami sandwich. You coming?"

Hank followed.

They ordered their food, and she paid for it, slipping into a booth while they waited for their order to be delivered to their table.

"Were you at the last game of the World Series when they won?" Hank asked.

Savannah opened her mouth, but then shut it.

"What's wrong with you lately?"

Savannah stared out the window. "I just made it up. I wasn't really here. Are you trying to catch me in a lie?"

Hank thought he already had, but he didn't answer. He felt like there was no use. She wasn't going to come clean on anything, and he'd only get madder.

"Do you believe what Brian said about Mr. Train and the tracks?" Savannah asked, not looking at Hank. "That girl out there has a pretty dress. Very retro."

Hank followed her gaze. "Is it retro if we're in 2034? Or is it the new fashion statement? Time is forgetful."

Their food came, and they ate in silence. Hank wanted to ask questions, but Savannah put her head down and ate like it was her last meal.

Hank wondered if it was going to be one of his last.

As soon as she was finished, Savannah cleared her side of the table and went to the bathroom.

Hank wondered why they were here, in this city at this time.

Who was the dwarf, Andy, really? Was Brian C. Redd telling them the truth? Anyone could have sent the letter. Hank felt like he was being played.

Savannah was back and looked like she'd lost her cat.

"You alright?" Hank asked, following her back on

the street.

"I'll be fine," Savannah said. "We should split up and see what we can find out. Cover more ground that way. I'll go east and south."

Hank shook his head. "That doesn't make any sense. We're in this together. We need to start to find the clues. They're never hard to see, and the two of us should be able to do it easily."

Savannah started walking in the direction they'd come. "I'm not going to argue with you, but you're wrong. We need to split up."

And then it hit him: Savannah. Too many coincidences. Too many times she'd come and go at the right time. She was part of this. She might even be the reason for his predicament.

Hank stopped her as they walked, pushing her roughly into a doorway.

"Tell me the truth," Hank said. "Enough is enough."

"I don't know what…"

Hank squeezed her shoulders, his fingers biting into her skin in his anger. He could see the lie in her eyes. He could see he'd been played from the moment he met her. "You. What part do you play in this? Tell me, or as God is my witness, I will kill you and leave your body in the nearest alley. It's all going to end in another day anyway. No one will even find your corpse."

"Are you okay?" a young man a few feet away stared at Savannah, and then glared at Hank. Under any other circumstances, Hank would have respected this kid immensely. Right now he wanted to kill him. They were all going to die soon anyway.

"It's a roleplay we do," Savannah said. "Mind your business."

The kid turned red and walked away quickly.

"Well?" Hank asked a little calmer.

"You aren't going to like it," she said, "but I can't explain everything you don't remember because you may not be done. There may be things you still need to do before you remember everything. I can't derail that, or this might all be for nothing."

"You're right. I don't like it, Savannah. What happened to not lying to each other, the one thing you made me promise when I patched up your shoulder?"

Savannah shook her head. "Please, don't do this. You'll only make it worse."

"Doubtful," Hank said. "Maybe I'm actually a serial killer. That's why I have no recollection of anything. I'm so evil my brain shuts down, compartmentalizes the awful things I do."

"You're not a serial killer," Savannah said.

Hank squeezed harder before he realized he was still holding her. "Then who am I? No more lies. You know. You've always known."

"Your name isn't Hank," Savannah said. She smiled, but it looked sad to him. "Obviously, that means my name isn't Savannah, either. I'm Mary."

Hank groaned. "If you tell me I'm Joseph, I'll scream."

She shook her head. "Your name is Brian… Brian C. Redd. If you complete what I think you're supposed to by tomorrow, it will extend the time by a full day." Now she was actually grinning. "Don't you see? We've moved it forward twenty-four hours. The world won't suddenly end at midnight, right as the ball drops to end 2034. There will actually be a 2035 now. Just as new days have been added all along."

"For one day? You mean we did all that for one lousy day?"

Savannah nodded. "One at a time, but yes. Unless I messed it all up again by telling you this much, and then we start over this loop from scratch, I guess."

"How can I be Brian? I've met him at least twice. Three times? Probably more. I don't look anything like him."

"Because the tracks were moved slightly. Enough to change small things about you, like who your parents are, who mine were. Not exactly a DNA match, but still the next version of us born forward in a new timeline we created each time around." Savannah shook her head. "I know you don't get it. I'm not explaining it well. I'm only just remembering. This is all very hard to take in. It's not a huge conspiracy."

"Who is Mr. Train? You know," Hank said. He wasn't Brian Redd. This was a mistake. He wasn't a writer, and he'd never wanted to be one. Had he? His head was hurting now. "If you changed my DNA, it would affect him, too."

"Not necessarily. There are multiple versions.

Remember? This version, the Hank version, is unique. Because it was … original." Savannah wasn't struggling, and Hank relaxed his grip, but kept his hands on her shoulders. "The same with me. There's other Marys out there. Many of them. A recent one I've seen is lonely. Frail. Unlike me. One time she went by Alice."

Saint Mary …

Hank remembered holding on to Savannah at another time and place. Holding on for dear life. Holding on to her because he loved her, and not because he hated her. There was something wildly important just at the edge of his memory.

A different Mary from a chance encounter popped into his head, and he somehow knew that was important, too.

Hank felt like he'd been punched in the gut. "I met a Mary… I met you… in Baltimore. In a bar waiting for her husband who'd left her."

Savannah teared up and nodded.

"Tell me what else you know," Hank said. He released her. He felt like a jerk for putting his hands on a woman.

Savannah sidestepped and was next to him on the sidewalk, looking around. "It isn't safe to do it this way. You have to finish your part. Whatever is still keeping you from remembering. What I have to do, you can't join me if you aren't finished. You'll understand later. I promise."

"Come on already… Mary."

"Tomorrow. I promise I'll give you all the answers before midnight tomorrow." Savannah wiped her eyes with the back of her hand. "With any luck, we'll be able to share the first day of 2035 together, too."

Hank sighed. It was like pulling teeth getting her to tell him the truth, and he knew she was done for today. She'd given him too much to think about, anyway.

"Who is Mr. Train?" Hank asked.

She took hold of him this time, supporting both sides of his face between her hands. "I trust you to do the right thing and I'm with you, however this turns out. If we're done with this loop, we'll move past it together. If we need to go back around the calendar again to get it right, I'll find you again, like we always do. If it's the end, really the end, then I'll face that with you, too. We're in this together even if you don't believe in me yet. If I had figured it out sooner, I would have told you."

He thought she was going to kiss him and then was disappointed when she let go of his face instead.

"Wait, Savannah … Mary."

Savannah turned away. "Tomorrow. Don't try to stop me. You won't see me until tomorrow night, depending on what you do leading up until that time." She glanced over her shoulder. "You do realize… you're the husband in the scenario in Baltimore? Another version of you that we created by doing this."

Chapter 33

December 31st, 2034 - San Francisco, California

Hank stepped off the transport back in San Francisco again. It was a much faster trip than it would have been in previous decades, but it was still took most of the day.

An old man walked up the sidewalk toward him, but Hank ignored him.

Hank had traveled out to Mesquite, Nevada to find Brian Redd's house leveled. The container was still there, but it was stripped bare. Wires had hung from the electrical, but nothing left of what had been there. If he was planning to publish a book in the coming year, he wasn't doing it from there. Looked like he wasn't splitting his time between Mesquite and Rusty Nail anymore, like his bio claimed.

Hank had raced to Salt Lake City next. The streets

and houses had changed from the last time he was there, and it was busy. The side of town he wanted to explore had people and traffic, and he suspected maybe there was another version of this region, maybe in another time, that existed apart from the world he was seeing now. Maybe it was a pocket universe. Maybe it was a bubble of time that existed as long as Savannah or Mary or whatever the hell her name was wanted it to exist.

This time period, this eve of destruction, was closing up shop. Perhaps there were timelines that went into subsequent years like Brian Redd had suggested, but this version of things was not preparing for that.

Even before he had reached that warehouse they had inspected in the 1980s not too many ports ago, he had known it would be as empty as Brian's writing trailer. He had reached the cracked parking lot to find it leveled, like Brian Redd's house. Weeds and scrub had the time to grow in the cleared sands where not a trace of the building remained.

"When they close shop, they close it up good," Hank had said.

He wanted to travel farther east to check out other sites he had visited. He wanted to see if the storage unit in New York still held his secrets. Maybe more nonsensical notebooks than before from more ports he didn't remember, more loops he'd failed to close, or that Savannah had erased from his mind, or Brian Redd had spiraled into some locked place in the back of his skull, or that some figure named Mr. Train had steered onto another track for his own reasons that maybe

Savannah/Mary understood, but withheld from him.

A Clocksmith agent, the last one before the end, could be waiting inside with a pistol and a shovel. *We got one grave left to dig, Hank. I need one more 138 button to complete my set.*

But travel restrictions had kept him from crossing the Mississippi River. The hired driver had fumbled and stuttered as he tried to explain the information on the transport's reader against Hank's profile from his thumbprint.

Hank had decided not to fight it. He had gone to Rusty Nail, Nevada instead.

He had sat on the bed in the room. The clothes, the money from different eras, and the supplies had still been there. Maybe the shop wasn't completely closed. He had been tempted to stay and wait out the end of the world there. Just let it all be over without Savannah or anyone else sending him back into the ringer with no memory of this new brush with the end.

Hank had caught himself looking around the room for clues. Old habits.

Then, he'd realized the temptation was something else. If he laid back on the bed and allowed his eyes to drift closed again, he would port. He'd known it. He wasn't certain what he would remember and what he wouldn't, but he knew he'd wake up in another time, in another place, in another room 138. Maybe that was what she wanted. That's what she meant when she said he wasn't finished. Maybe he had done this exact thing on a hundred New Year's Eves before. But then, maybe she wanted him to do the opposite and return to her in San Francisco just like she had claimed.

One more time around the calendar … I'll find you … like we always do.

He had wondered how long the transport driver would wait for him if he did port right out of this era. Would he wait right up until the new end of the world, however long that took?

His fingers had tingled, and his head had spun. The energy of the port had pulsed through him. He recalled porting while standing up, at least once before. It had happened in a club once that he remembered. It was possible it was about to happen now, whether he wanted it or not.

He had stood up and staggered away from the bed and then lurched for the door. The unbalanced pull of the port clung to him and pulled at him, even after he staggered into the hall before the door was done sliding silently open. Hank had leaned against the wall to keep from falling to the floor.

As he had stared back through the open door, he wanted there to be some message. A note from a future or past version of himself telling him what to do next, how to foil Savannah and Mr. Train's plans for good. He'd even be happy with a video from an alternate version of himself that had figured out the game long before this Hank version of himself had. Some recruit out of some timeline where he was born different, smarter, stronger, faster, or wiser needed to appear and let Hank know what needed to be done next to break whatever this thing was for good.

For the first time he could recall, he wanted someone else to be in control. That was new.

Or better yet, a superspy version of Hank Brian Redd Smith needed to tap his shoulder and say, *"It's okay, Buddy. You played your part. You did fine. I got it from here. Go lie down and rest. You've earned it. Just one more port for you. I'll set everything right, and then you'll wake up back in your home, in your time, like nothing happened. You'll remember your name, your wife's name, and your kids' names, and it will be like you were never gone. You'll appreciate them and your real life even more now because of all you have been through, and in time, the memories of what you have suffered will fade as new and better memories are made in the normal flow of time."*

Hank had waited in that hallway a long time. Long after the pull of the port had faded, he had waited. But nothing like that had happened. No messages and no saviors arrived.

"Looks like I have to be in control after all," Hank had said out loud. "If I am in control, I'm going to want more than one damn day for all this trouble."

He had finally left, and the driver had brought him back to San Francisco without Hank knowing much more than when he left.

The old man, on the sidewalk where the transport had dropped Hank off, reached him as Hank's mind wandered. Hank stepped back absently toward the curb to let the man pass, but instead of passing, the old guy grabbed Hank by the throat with both hands.

Hank went off balance and grabbed a light post with one hand to keep from spilling to his back in the street. He met the old man's eyes, looking into one blue eye and one green eye.

Chapter 34

December 31st, 2034 - San Francisco, California

Was this the same Clocksmith from 1975? Hank wondered if the guy still had the pocket knife Hank had dropped six decades ago. Or maybe he had upgraded to something deadlier.

Another old man stepped up from the other direction and shoved the strange-eyed Clocksmith away from Hank. The man staggered, but didn't fall as he heaved for air.

A young man stepped up for Savannah; an old man steps up for me.

In the lull, Hank recognized Brian C. Redd. He was older than the other times he had seen him. He had shaved, which helped his look a little. He looked good for his age, but he looked every bit of his late eighties, pushing a healthy ninety.

The old man with two different colored eyes pointed at Hank with a boney finger. "Unnatural. You will be stopped. Not by me, but by someone, sometime. You will."

His finger shook for a moment longer, and then he hobbled away.

That was it.

Hank and Brian watched for a long time, until the guy disappeared around the corner to finish out his days doing whatever the hell elder Clocksmiths did in their off time.

I never did figure out what that group was all about.

"Thanks, I guess?" Hank said.

Brian chuckled. "Yeah, you're welcome, I guess. That wasn't nearly as harrowing as I expected. Clocksmiths … what a bunch of twits."

"You got me to San Francisco. Not sure what the hell I'm supposed to do now."

Brian chuckled again. "I'm sorry I bailed on you."

"What do you mean?"

Brian waved a finger in the air. "The whole 138 mission. Didn't remember what we were doing at the time. By the time I had locked myself into the flow of time, it was too late to return to the cause."

"I don't know what you're talking about," Hank said. "Savannah says you and I are the same person."

"Cut from the same cloth," Brian said, "but each our own person. It's sad to realize at this point every time around the timeline that I'm out of the loop. Each time you guys succeed, it just ends for me, but I'm there in time when you start over, not even realizing what it's all about. I guess in a sense, I'm living on, too. I'm a part of history in my own way. I still play my part. I helped you guys, didn't I? You only freaked out and punched me once."

"I guess you helped us." Hank shook his head. "What am I supposed to remember?"

"Oh," Brian said. "You're still figuring it out? Maybe it's not done. I thought this loop was over."

"Tell me what it means."

Brian sighed. "You and Savannah will figure it out together faster than I could explain it from my limited perspective. It'll make sense soon, and then everything will be fine. You'll see."

Hank turned away. "I need to find her."

"You will. You two always do. Tell her and everyone I'll miss them."

"What is there to miss, Brian? I don't even remember."

"I won't be here to see how it ends. How you two save it all again."

"Does it end, Brian? Seems like it loops around forever and ever."

"Progress is always hard won," Brian said. "When you do go back around to buy another day for the world, I'll be there in time, in my little houses, writing my little books, with no idea what I gave up not being a 138 anymore. Keep sending me the messages, and I'll keep helping when you need it."

"It was a dumb code, Brian."

Brian gave a laugh that was more breath than voice. "It's good to stay in touch with your friends. Even those of us trapped in time while you do all the heavy lifting out here."

"I think I'm done, too," Hank said.

Brian smiled and patted Hank's shoulder. "Then, it was always a pleasure every time around, sir."

Brian C. Redd left to enjoy what remained of 2034 and all of history on his own.

Hank had no idea where to find her, or even if he had decided he really wanted to. He searched the streets until he couldn't feel his wet feet in the cold any longer. He finally stopped shivering and thought maybe this was it. He had read somewhere, maybe in a Brian C. Redd novel, that you could get hypothermia at temperatures as high as fifty degrees Fahrenheit if it was wet or windy enough. San Francisco was both that evening.

He found people, but not Savannah. He stayed among them to block the wind and to steal some warmth. In the clusters of the crowd, he found tall heaters set up, blowing out heat. He didn't realize how cold he had gotten until he huddled with the others near those heaters. Hank started to shiver again as he warmed up in the darkness of the street and the bright lights of the buildings above.

The countdown started.

He looked up at the giant screens flashing down in digital numbers at a Colossus scale. Hank didn't realize he had wandered around all the way to midnight Pacific Time. He could have looked to see what had happened in other time zones, as what could be the last midnight swept the face of the Earth back around to him. Most of the world had entered the New Year and had done so in a way that alarmed none of these people. But he hadn't looked up any of that information. He was a time traveler now totally unaware of time.

The titan numbers flashed down in time with the chants of the worshipful crowd. Like God carving his commandments with a fiery finger, the countdown reached one.

Savannah grabbed Hank by the lapels of his coat and pulled him around to face her. His bag with the 138 button on the strap bounced against his side. He stared into her eyes above her cheeks flushed red from the cold air.

Time froze, but not metaphorically. The screens froze in a glitched transition between one and zero. The crowd locked into place waiting for the end without realizing they were doing it. Only he and she still moved apart from the natural flow of time which had ceased to move in any direction in that moment.

Her voice carried through the timeless air over the short distance between them in a jagged echo, but he heard every word while understanding none of them. "You are Mr. Train, and it has been hell trying to follow your orders this time around. I'm sorry I wasn't nicer to you. Thank you for not giving up on me."

She pulled him into a kiss and time crashed back into motion, loud and painful. It was the opposite of a port. Instead of swirling and fading, he was hyper present and every sensation, right down to the cold wetness of his feet and the soft warmth of her lips against his, was too real.

The crowd screamed zero.

Cheers erupted.

Fireworks exploded.

Music clamored from a dozen competing sources.

The year ended.

The two of them traveled into the next year connected together.

He knew his name again.

And he remembered everything.

Chapter 35

January 1st, 2035 - San Francisco, California

They entered the hotel lobby, and a couple stood up to greet them. Hank was fixated on the large circular sign on the wall above the conference room doors in front of them. 138 stood out bold on the red, white, and blue circle like a massive campaign button.

Clocksmiths staying in this hotel must be losing their ever-loving minds right now.

Savannah said, "This is Mary and Brian Redd. Our new recruits for the next loop. They both turned thirty-eight today. Can you believe it?"

"I could believe most anything." Hank shook their hands.

This Mary was tall and blond. Not as fragile as some versions they had recruited after previous cycles. Time would tell how strong she really was.

This Brian Redd was shorter and broader than

Hank, not quite as short as the dwarf, though. That had been an unusual recruitment, but Andy had proven quite capable, hadn't he?

"Sorry I wasn't there for your intake," Hank said.

"We understand," Mary Redd said.

Did she? Did she have any idea what they had agreed to?

Each cycle, a new version of this pair was born. Sometimes they found each other before becoming 138s. Sometimes that came later.

"It's time," Hank said.

Together the four of them entered the room marked with a giant 138.

He was going to be Hank from this moment forward, however many moments they had left. Except… when they ported tonight, right before midnight, he would become someone else. They all would take another name, become a new person, and dive back into the timestream again.

To save the world another day. To move the needle twenty-four hours into the future.

He was Mr. Train. He had been Hank Smith for a little over ten cycles of years this time. It had been a rough loop this time around. There was no tomorrow, at least, not yet.

"We do these things so there will be another day of light and darkness," Hank said to those gathered in the hotel conference room with him.

All of them were here. All who had survived. Even

with the 138ers from overseas, there were a couple dozen left out of thousands of recruits. Thousands upon thousands.

Andy, "the dwarf," was here. No one could kill him, it seemed. Mary from the Baltimore bar was here, but never found her husband. He wasn't going to make it for another loop. The kid from the storage unit who had been all confused when Hank met him, Adam was the name he had gone by this time around. He was a good recruit. A man with a black leather jacket and long hair, Matt O'Leary from the Nashville bar, he had a new guitar case with him instead of his satchel.

Each cycle, a new pair of them were born, a new version capable of porting, and they were recruited into the cause.

"We lost a lot this time around. Good people. Alice, Terry, Barbara …" Hank remembered her scar. She was tough, had been porting for many loops, and would be missed. " … Avery, Ethan, Bethany …" The names went on, but he took the time to name them all.

It had all come back, and it was mind-numbing to have all of the information at once in his head. Not just who these people were, who he truly was, but all of the stored information in the world, past and present and small future, from so many loops, buying so many days.

Savannah, his Mary Redd, took his hand as he paused after the last name. She smiled at him. She had been his wife in another time, in all times.

"The Clocksmiths were an unexpected wrinkle this

time around. I'm not sure how that changes when we start again. They might vanish. A new group might take their place. We might make them worse, but what we do matters."

Andy said, "Oh, we can take those bums."

Everyone laughed.

"We start again in Galveston. September 8, 1900," Hank said.

That got everyone quiet.

Savannah wasn't smiling now. "The hurricane. The beginning for us. Are you sure you want to start there? What about where this really began? October 1962? Wouldn't that make more sense? When the world was ripped apart in nuclear holocaust the first time?"

Hank shook his head. "We've been going about this all wrong. We're so geared toward changing the one event, the end of the world, that we're neglecting so many other disasters. Why?"

Andy raised his hand. "We've added over seventy years to the lifespan of the planet and the human race so far. We've also managed to stop half a dozen other blunders that should've ended the world. The Cuban one was just the start. Yet... aren't we just pushing up the inevitable? Someday, somewhere, someone is going to push the button and nuke the rest of the world or let out another superbug we can't stop. Then it will all be for nothing." He stood. "We need to be more proactive."

Hank shook his head. He'd heard this argument

before. Nearly every loop, on the last day they'd been able to push forward, they had this caucus. A meeting of the surviving players and the wide-eyed new recruits in this dance. "We will not change history by killing those who would try to destroy it. That is not our mission."

"How do you know?" Andy was staring at Hank. He had been at this a long time and deserved his say. "Mr. Train, with all due respect, this is even bigger than you. While our work is amazing, and it truly touches billions of lives, it's at such a snail's pace, and… one day there will be too many threats to overcome. Years' worth of porting through time to pull strings, move people into certain situations and change small, minor details in order to gain another day… doesn't seem worth it anymore. Over seventy years of this. Over twenty-five thousand days gained by doing this for nearly ten million days." Andy shook his head.

"It's a little over twenty-six thousand days we've gained and closer to a hundred million days of work to get there." Hank shrugged. Everyone laughed lightly again. "Not all the loops took a decade of porting to complete, but this was a tough one, a tiring one, I admit. But we're not going to lie down and let the world end."

The crowd mumbled their agreement.

Andy rolled his eyes, but smiled. "If we remembered everything, it'd be easier. You'd at least remember to call me a little person instead of a dwarf or a midget this time."

"I think that was my fault this time," Savannah said.

Andy's smile wavered. "I was kidding. You were

angry about Alice. So was I. She figured out how to disconnect enough to start aging again, but not enough to stop porting. It drove her crazy, made her vulnerable, and got her killed."

"I'm sorry," Savannah whispered.

"I am, too." Andy stared at the floor. "I hate that I'm going to forget her again when we leave here."

"If we remembered everything, we'd go insane and never know what to change," Hank said. "I understand the frustration, but it has to be clear-minded, and the clues that come from that open state of mind, the instincts that come from our power to do this. We were all born with a special gift and a special power that allows for this work. It comes with a responsibility to oversee and protect time. We will do it and find a way to do it better now."

Savannah smiled. "I love it. Well, sometimes I love it. The adventure. The intrigue. Not knowing what comes next. Trying to figure out who we are, and what part we play in this. Remembering before you and having to wait for you to catch up." She winked. "I'm ready to get my mind wiped and get my first port in, honey. This time can I be Atlanta? You can call me Lanny."

A few of them started to murmur and Mr. Train - Hank - Brian put his hands in the air. The room went silent.

"In 1900, on September 8th, in my first life, I was a small child. The Great Galveston Storm came ashore and wiped us out. It was estimated to be at least a Category 4. The worst hurricane in our history, in terms of loss of life and property. The city was close to being completely wiped out and destroyed. The estimate is between six and twelve thousand people died." He sighed. "The tidal surge was fifteen feet. We were only five feet above sea level. It tore through the city like it was made of paper."

He knew they had been expecting the story; he almost always told it at this point, loop after loop, and the spot they normally started: the Cuban Missile Crisis, where the world came to an end in a flash of nuclear explosions that wiped out humanity the first time. They'd successfully pushed that end day back seventy years, but it wasn't enough.

"My first memories are of that storm and living as an orphan at St. Mary's. The nuns tried to save us. They tied themselves to us children, hoping their strength and belief in God would shield them from the water and the wind. Only two of us escaped."

He pulled Savannah, his Mary, closer to him. "We survived because we ported, but wouldn't understand that power until years later, when a World War jarred our power to life again. We started figuring out what we could do, and that we could change things as we moved. Then, we realized the different versions of us born in the new timelines we created could do this, too. Then, you joined us." He pointed at Andy and O'Leary. Their Marys had been lost, Andy's partner this time around and Matt's Mary several loops ago.

Hank pulled Savannah in even tighter.

"We've never started back so far," Savannah said.

"Do you suppose it will help us? Do you think it will make the time we gain go faster?"

"I don't know what it will do," Hank admitted. "I just know it needs to be done."

Everyone stood when Hank motioned for them to rise. He knew there were some who were sick of playing this game, and wanted a normal life.

Brian C. Redd the author says he misses you all, but do you envy him?

Where would this all end? He didn't know. It was his lot in life, such as it was, to do this.

"I'm going to wipe your memories. All of your independent thoughts connected to mine as we set the tracks in place for another loop to create more time for the world. We will tie ourselves together and face the storm as one, while we save those innocent people counting on us for a longer life," he said. He had his arms raised. "Close your eyes and think of a name. One you haven't used before. One you want to wake up tomorrow and be known as."

They all closed their eyes, including Hank… who was now going to be known as Isaac.

"Make sure you grab your new satchel on your way out the door. There are lots of room 138s in town waiting for us to begin again."

Jay Wilburn is a kidney transplant recipient and a very slow long-distance runner. He is the author of books like the Maidens of Zombie Kingdom books, the Vampire Christ Trilogy, the Dead Song series, and more. You can find him streaming writing live at Twitch.tv/JayWilburn or see videos on the topic of writing at his Captain Three Kidneys YouTube Channel.

Armand Rosamilia is a New Jersey boy currently living in sunny Florida, where he writes when he's not sleeping. He's happily married to a woman who helps his career and is supportive, which is all he ever wanted in life...

He's written over 150 stories that are currently available, including horror, zombies, contemporary fiction, thrillers and more. His goal is to write a good story and not worry about genre labels.Arm Cast Podcast - interviewing fellow authors as well as filmmakers, musicians, etc.

He also loves to talk in third person... because he's really that cool.

You can find him at https://armandrosamilia.com for not only his latest releases but interviews and guest posts with other authors he likes!

MORE BOOKS FROM

EXTINCTION PEAK
BY LUCAS MANGUM

THE REATTACHMENT
BY DOUGLAS FORD

A BAPTISM FOR THE DEAD
BY CHARLES BERNARD

LAND SHARK
BY ALEX GONZALEZ

ALL MEN ARE TRASH
BY GINA RINALLI

A Madness Heart Press Publication

9 781734 893755